Evan took her hand, his fingers lightly lacing into hers.

Anna was shaken by the sizzle of heat that flared from that simple touch. Stiffening her spine, she stared at him directly, refusing to look away this time. She knew he was playing with her; he teased her every chance he got. Why was it so hard to keep herself from taking it seriously?

"Come on. What do you want, Evan?" she asked, keeping her voice even with effort. "Stop playing around and spill it."

His gaze flickered down to her mouth for a second, then lifted back to her eyes. The emerald depths drew her into their heat and promise. "It's simple," he said softly. "I want *you*, Annie."

Dear Reader,

This is my third book about the Berzanis, a family living, laughing and loving on the shores of the Chesapeake Bay. Evan McKenzie has been around from the beginning, having been Patrick Berzani's best friend since the age of twelve. From the moment he slid his sunglasses down his nose in the first story and winked at me, I was hooked. A bad boy in a sharp suit, he is every woman's fantasy—and nightmare. But there had to be more to him than charming arrogance and a sarcastic wit. Otherwise, why would the Berzanis love him? And what had happened to Evan's own family?

I had a hint of the answers when I saw how he supported Patrick in his quest for happiness. Another came the first time I watched Evan and Anna Berzani snap at each other. There *was* more here than met the eye. I hope you enjoy finding out the truth about Evan McKenzie as much as I did.

Please visit me at www.lisaruff.net. And keep a watch out for my next book from Harlequin.

Happy reading,

Lisa Ruff

Baby Bombshell
LISA RUFF

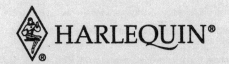

HARLEQUIN®

TORONTO • NEW YORK • LONDON
AMSTERDAM • PARIS • SYDNEY • HAMBURG
STOCKHOLM • ATHENS • TOKYO • MILAN • MADRID
PRAGUE • WARSAW • BUDAPEST • AUCKLAND

Recycling programs
for this product may
not exist in your area.

ISBN-13: 978-0-373-75321-5

BABY BOMBSHELL

Copyright © 2010 by Lisa Ruff.

ABOUT THE AUTHOR

Lisa Ruff grew up in Idaho. The daughter of a forester, she lived in small towns nestled deep in the mountains. Lisa met the man of her dreams in Seattle. She married Kirk promising to love, honor and edit his rough drafts. His writing led Lisa, a longtime reader of romance, to the craft.

Seeking time to write, Lisa, Kirk and their cat sailed from Seattle on a 37-foot boat. They spent five years cruising, living an adventurous life. Lisa kept busy writing travel essays, learning to speak Spanish from taxi drivers and handling a small boat in gale-force winds on the ocean.

Finally, after fifteen years afloat, Lisa and her husband live on land in Philadelphia. In an apartment overlooking the Delaware River, she is busy writing.

Books by Lisa Ruff

HARLEQUIN AMERICAN ROMANCE

1214—MAN OF THE YEAR
1243—BABY ON BOARD
1303—UNEXPECTED FATHER

For Mary: thanks for being Italian

Chapter One

Anna Berzani bent over the drafting table, spreading a layer of vellum over the site plan. Her laptop sat open next to her, flashing the photos she had taken while visiting the site. Sketching quickly, she outlined her idea for the new building, translating the vision in her head from three dimensions to two. She could see the contours of the land cradling the glass, steel and concrete. Resting her chin on her fist for a moment, she considered the drawing before curving one line and changing the angle on another.

"Nice view."

Anna froze. Her pencil fell to the table. She knew that deep voice with the thread of amusement running through it. But it couldn't be him—it *couldn't*. He was three thousand miles away. Slowly, she turned her head, looking over her shoulder to the door.

A tall man stood smiling at her from the doorway of her office. He was gorgeous: his jaw chiseled, nose arrow-straight. His short blond hair gleamed like old gold under the harsh florescent lights. Anna's fingers itched to touch it, to thread through the silken strands. Beneath the perfectly tailored suit he wore, she knew his shoulders were broad, tapering to a narrow waist. Probably well tanned, too; the memory of him standing on the dock in the hot summer sunshine in nothing but swim trunks made her mouth go dry. His casual stance—hands tucked into the pockets of his gray suit trousers—made him look like a model from a glossy magazine: fashionable, smooth and slightly dangerous.

In seconds, she was snared by laughing green eyes, mischief radiating from them, luring her in. *The man of my dreams,* Anna thought hazily as she straightened and turned toward him, pulled by some unbidden force. He walked to her, holding her eyes captive with his. Her breath caught as he leaned over and kissed her on the cheek. The feel of his warm lips on her skin sent a shiver down her spine.

"How's it going, Anna-Banana?"

Anna cringed at the nickname and came back to reality with a bump. "Now I remember why I never miss you," she said tartly.

Evan McKenzie laughed. "Oh, you miss me," he said, tapping a finger on her chin. "You just won't admit it."

"What are you doing here?"

"I was in the neighborhood, so I thought I'd stop by."

"Liar."

Anna folded her arms and leaned back against the table with a studied nonchalance that belied her inner turmoil. Her heart was thudding crazily and she felt as if there wasn't enough air in the room. She wanted to move away from Evan—the next state wouldn't be too far—but that risked revealing how much he had unsettled her. She knew better than to show any weakness.

Evan shook his head. "You're a hard woman to fool, Anna Berzani."

"And don't you ever forget it." Anna tilted her head to one side. "How did you get in here, anyway? I'm supposed to have a secretary out there to intercept intruders like you."

Evan walked over to her desk and picked up a paperweight. As he shook the small globe, sparkles of color shifted and whirled around a miniature Golden Gate Bridge. He grinned and slid a glance over at Anna.

"She's a lovely woman. Very helpful. I'd give her a generous bonus."

"Meaning you smarmed your way past her." Refusing to be charmed herself, Anna shook her head in exasperation. She didn't hold her secretary's laxness against her. Evan McKenzie could sell honey to bees and coax the stars from heaven.

"Oh, Annie," he said with a frown, setting the globe down and turning to face her. "You shouldn't be so cynical. Besides, I'm not an intruder, I'm practically *family*."

Anna snorted. "Not hardly."

"Your mother claims me."

"She's never been very discriminating."

Evan walked back over to stand directly in front of Anna again.

Despite her best efforts, she felt a flush of color mount her cheeks as his gaze traveled over her face. This close to him, she could smell the faint aroma of his aftershave—citric and sharp—with another underlying scent that was Evan alone. Dropping her eyes, she focused on the neatly knotted yellow paisley tie at his throat. When he reached out an arm, she tensed in anticipation—of what, she didn't know.

"Where's this?"

His hand slipped past her, pointing to her computer. Lashes flying up, Anna realized he was looking at the screen of her laptop, not at her. The click of the mouse as he scrolled through her photos sounded loud to her ears. Cursing herself, she willed her heart to settle to a safe, steady pace.

"Arcata. I'm designing a resort."

"Beautiful site. What kind?"

"It's primarily for company retreats, but there's a full spa along with three pools, a gym and two restaurants that will be open to the public, too." Anna shifted away from Evan to look at the pictures—any excuse to put some distance between them. "I'm going to site the building overlooking the valley. The corner will go here, with balconies out this way." She tapped her pencil on the rough sketch she had done.

Evan looked at the paper, his eyes narrowed. "Yes, and if this line curved in over here, you could hide that pool behind this clump of trees. It would make it more private."

Anna frowned as she absorbed his observation. Looking down at the drawing, she realized he had a point. She penciled in his suggestion with a few quick strokes. It would work surprisingly well. Adding a couple extra shrubs at the base of the trees, she cocked her head to one side, contemplating the change. *Yes. And that would make this part of the building—*

"Don't worry. I won't tell anyone that you got help from an unlicensed amateur," Evan said with a chuckle.

Anna glanced up to find him watching her. She flushed again and put down the pencil. "Why *are* you here bugging me, anyway?" she asked irritably.

Evan's eyelids lowered for a moment. When they lifted, all laughter had vanished, as if a shutter had been drawn over his thoughts. Anna couldn't read his expression now and that worried her. What *did* he want? He would not have flown across the entire country on a whim. There was a reason for him to be in San Francisco. She just had to figure out what it was and send him back to Maryland.

Startling her from her thoughts, Evan took her hand,

his fingers lightly lacing into hers. Anna was shaken by
the sizzle of heat that flared from that simple touch. Stiffening her spine, she stared at him, refusing to look away
this time. She knew he was playing with her; he teased her
every chance he got. Why was it so hard to keep herself
from taking it seriously?

"Come on. What do you want, Evan?" she asked, keeping her voice even with effort. "Stop playing around and
spill it."

His gaze flickered down to her mouth for a second, then
lifted back to her eyes. The emerald depths drew her into
their heat and promise. "It's simple," he said softly. "I want
you, Annie."

Anna pulled her hand from his. Reaching back, she
gripped the edge of the worktable, searching for some solid
foundation in a suddenly teetering world. The words were a
shock. She had waited a long time to hear them—thirteen
years, to be exact—ever since she was fifteen years old.
She swallowed hard, her throat dry.

"Here's your coffee, Mr. McKenzie. I'm sorry it took so
long, but I made a fresh pot for you."

Anna jerked as the bright voice of her secretary cut
through the haze in her brain. Evan kept his gaze locked
to hers for another moment longer, then turned to face the
other woman. Anna sucked in a deep breath. The hard edge
of the table bit into her palms, bringing some measure of
sanity. What the hell had just happened?

"You didn't have to do that, Sarah," Evan said. "Thank
you."

"Oh, no problem," she said with a chirp. "Can I get you
anything else?"

"Not a thing. This is more than enough."

Anna watched the exchange in silence, glad for the respite. She used the opportunity to slide past Evan and walk

around her desk, again putting distance between herself and Evan McKenzie. She sat in her chair, grateful to get off her wobbly legs, and stared blindly at the papers strewn across the desk.

Once, she had had a crush on Evan McKenzie. Her older brother's best friend, he had been a constant visitor to their house, a fixture in her life for years. She didn't know when it had happened exactly, but she had gradually come to realize that she was in love with him. He, of course, hardly knew that she was alive. Well, she corrected herself, he knew she was *there,* he just didn't know she was female. Five years older, Evan had not been interested in a skinny redheaded girl, the little sister in his adopted family.

His indifference hadn't spared her from heartache; it only intensified the pain. She had watched longingly as he paraded a series of girlfriends past her, wishing all the time she could be the one he touched, cuddled and kissed. The only attention he granted young Anna was merciless teasing, the sort with which any brother tormented his little sister. Eventually, Anna left for college, giving her the chance to outgrow her crush. Time and distance had cured her. She had thought they had. Until today.

Anna looked up at Evan. He was turned away from her, but she saw Sarah backing out of the office, still smiling and chattering. Her secretary's face bloomed rosy with blushes he had no doubt cultivated.

Sighing, she rubbed a hand over her forehead. Somehow, his sudden appearance had caused her to slip back to the age when she was young and too hopeful. She didn't want to be that aching teenager again. She wasn't in love with Evan McKenzie now. God knew, Evan would never be in love with her. As far as she knew, he had never been in love with *any* woman.

Evan set his mug down on Anna's desk. "Why the fierce

look, Annie? Does your secretary making coffee for me
offend your feminist principles?"

Anna frowned, then flicked a hand in a dismissive gesture. "That's her business. No one orders anyone around
here. We all pitch in to get the work done, whatever the
job requires."

"How egalitarian of you." Evan sat in the chair across
from her, hitching up his pant legs and settling himself
comfortably. He looked relaxed and cool, everything Anna
wasn't.

She leaned back in her chair, forcing herself to act un-
perturbed. "And speaking of jobs, I ought to get back to
mine."

"Ah, but you *are* working. You're meeting with a potential client right now." When Evan smiled, Anna tensed
even more.

"You?" she asked, her eyes narrowing on his face. "I
thought you just bought a new house."

"No. It's bigger than that. Much bigger."

"Does this involve Patrick in some way?"

Evan tilted his head. "It might." His face was innocence
personified. "Why'd you ask?"

Anna snorted in derision. "I'm not getting snared into
one of your schemes. Every stunt you guys dream up usually ends in disaster of some kind."

"Give us a chance, Annie," he said, his eyes alight with
mischief once more. "You haven't heard the details."

"I don't need to. I've experienced some of the *details*
before," Anna said drily. "Remember that submarine idea
you two cooked up?"

"We were kids then."

"And you're *so* mature now." She shook her head. "Patty
should have known I'd say no, Evan. Is that why he sent
you to do the dirty work?"

"He thinks I can be more persuasive in this particular situation," Evan said with a smirk.

"I see." She tapped a pencil on the desk. "Just out of curiosity, what big idea are we talking about?" she asked. If she was wise, she would skip the question and get rid of him. Immediately.

"Nothing special. Just redeveloping your parents' property."

"What?" Anna stared at him. Of all the possibilities, this was the last thing she expected him to say. "The boatyard? Into *what?*"

"Anything but a boatyard. It's a beautiful location," Evan said. "Perfect for a few condos, some retail, maybe even a restaurant."

"But what about the business?" Anna asked, bewildered.

"We definitely keep the marina. It'll be a real draw once we get all the other stuff in place." Evan leaned forward. "Here's the deal. First, you do the design. Next stop is the planning commission, which should be a slam dunk, and we're in business. We could break ground by March first."

"Wait a minute here," Anna said, holding up one hand. "March *first?* It's August, Evan."

"I know it's pushing it, but we can do it, Annie."

"You're nuts." Anna shook her head. "Even if I—"

"Okay, we don't have to break ground by March," Evan said. "But we *have* to get the planning commission stamp by November first. After that we can relax the schedule."

"November?" Anna's voice rose to a squeak. The man was insane. *"What* is the rush?"

"Funding," he said, his green eyes intent as they stared into hers. "There's a temporary federal program, the Small Community Development Fund, to help encourage projects like this one. We qualify and honestly, we can't do the project without that money. But it expires sooner than we thought."

Anna's head was spinning from all the information Evan had thrown at her. The fact that her parents wanted to redevelop the boatyard was the first mystery, but she set that aside for the moment. She had to nip this craziness in the bud.

"It's completely unrealistic. First off, the planning process alone is likely to take months."

"I have a connection on the commission. Miriam Shermer. She's a pretty strong voice. If we give her plans and applications, she'll get us the approval we need in time."

"Even still, there's a lot to be done before you apply for permits, like site surveys, traffic studies, a public comment period. And all that takes place *after* the design is worked out."

"That's why I'm here. You know the property, the area and, most important, the clients," he countered smoothly. "You can put together a design your parents will love in no time at all, Annie."

"That's presuming my parents even know what they want."

"Since when does your father *not* have an opinion about anything?"

"Knowing my father, he probably has ten opinions, all contradictory to each other," Anna said with a snap, then gave an irritated sigh. "This is ridiculous. I haven't lived in Crab Creek for eleven years, Evan. I have no idea what's being built out there. I'd have to dig through all the local ordinances for restrictions, variances, zoning. Besides that, I'm not licensed in Maryland."

"Don't worry," he said, waving a hand in dismissal. "I

know an architect who's willing to do a reciprocal stamp for you. Whatever you don't know, he can fill in the gaps."

"Then why aren't you using him?"

"Because we want you."

"Well, you can't have me," Anna said tartly. Silly as it seemed, refusing him helped her regain some of her equilibrium. She had found a toehold and she wasn't going to let him knock her off balance again. Eyeing him, suspicion began to percolate through her brain. "How did you get Ma and Pop to agree to this, anyway?"

"They're not as inflexible as you like to think they are," Evan said impatiently. "They know the property's going to waste as it is. Do you know what houses are selling for around there? And George Green got an offer for his bar that—"

A buzz from her phone cut his words off midstream. Anna picked up the handset, grateful for the interruption. "Yes?"

"Anna, it's Carl. Do you have a minute? Ed and I are going over the plans for the Jepsen project, and we have a few glitches you might be able to help us with."

"I'll be there as soon as I can." Anna hung up the phone and looked over at Evan. "I'm going to have to kick you out."

"So we'll meet later—"

Anna held up a hand to stop him. "I don't see the point. I'm not interested in this job. For one, I have way too much on my plate as it is."

"Come on, Annie. We *need* you."

"If you don't want to use a local architect," she said, ignoring his plea, "I can recommend someone else."

"You're really turning me down?" Evan's face was unreadable again, eyes narrowed.

"I really am." Anna folded her hands on her desk. "You and Patty will have to look elsewhere."

"What can I say to change your mind?"

"Not a thing, Evan." She stood and he followed suit. "Goodbye. I'm sorry you made the trip for nothing."

"Oh, it hasn't been wasted." Evan smiled slyly. "Not yet."

With that, he turned and walked out of her office. Anna watched him go down the hall. She rubbed the back of her neck, feeling a knot of tension. His last words sounded a lot like a threat. She knew him too well: Evan was not one to give up so easily. But nothing he could say would change her mind.

EVAN PUSHED THROUGH THE revolving doors, exiting the building with a muttered curse. He walked to the edge of the sidewalk, then looked up to Anna's office, high above the street. "Don't think this is over, Anna-Banana. I'm not leaving San Francisco until you say 'yes.'"

A man in a dark suit slowed and stared at him. Evan raised an eyebrow in cold inquiry and the man hurried away. With a harsh sigh, Evan turned and walked down the street, his fists in his pockets. How the hell was he going to convince her now? His cell phone rang and he pulled it out, groaning when he saw Patrick's number on the screen.

"What do you want?"

"So the big deal guy got shot down," Patrick said.

"It's *Master Deal-maker,* thank you."

"Whatever. Anna just called and blasted me. What happened?"

"First recon mission accomplished. Preliminary strategic data on target collected."

"Come on, Evan. You blew the mission, buddy. The

target is pissed." Patrick sighed. "I knew this was a bad idea."

"A bad idea? You're the idiot that came up with it!" Evan stopped dead on the sidewalk, the pedestrian behind him snarling as she swerved to avoid collision. He pulled the speaker from his ear. Since his best friend was not there to punch, he wanted to chuck the phone across the street. He brought the phone back and said furiously, *"'Go talk to Anna, Evan. You're the man. You haven't lost a deal yet.'"*

"And you fell for it, sucker. You owe me a hundred bucks."

"I haven't lost the bet. Not *yet.* I'm just getting warmed up."

"From what Anna said to me, she's not going to say yes now or a hundred years from now."

"My plane doesn't leave until tomorrow morning," Evan reminded him. "I've got seventeen hours to change her mind."

Patrick was silent for a long moment. "So what's the *Master Deal-maker*'s next big move?"

"That's classified information. Need-to-know basis only. I'll report back to HQ tomorrow. In person." Evan flipped the phone off and dropped it in his pocket.

Brave words, he thought as he meandered down the street. Now he just had to come up with the deeds to back them up. He walked toward his hotel, then, still stewing, continued on past it, down to the Embarcadero. The weather was sunny, mild, glorious, not what he expected for San Francisco, even in the middle of August. He had assumed there would be lots of fog, wind and a damp chill. Instead, it was a welcome change from the heat and humidity of the Chesapeake summer.

He crossed the broad boulevard and made his way to

the ferry terminal. Threading his way through the waiting cars, he took out his cell phone and snapped a picture of Gandhi's statue. Walking over to the pier's edge, he took another photo of a ferry arriving, just to prove he had been here. It was probably all the sightseeing he would get on this quick trip.

Standing at the edge of the water, he leaned his elbows on the steel railing. A light breeze from the Bay blew into his face, bringing with it the crisp, tangy scent of the Pacific. Eyes narrowed against the sparkle of light off the water, Evan considered his options. He could go back to her office and try again, but that would no doubt fail; Anna was too businesslike sitting behind her desk. In that setting, she felt in charge and could say no too easily. He had also hammered on the business side of their plans too much. A more personal approach might be a better tactic. He needed to get her to relax, away from her own turf. Distract her, then hit her with both barrels.

The prospect of getting personal with Anna Berzani sent a flash of heat through his veins. Evan reined it in instantly, with an ease that spoke of years of practice. The first time he had felt that spark had been the summer she turned sixteen. Anna had pranced around in a bikini that left little to the imagination. It had nearly killed him, but at twenty-one, he knew he couldn't touch her; she was jailbait for certain. Besides, she was his best friend's sister. If he made a move, Patrick would have killed him, or worse.

That summer had been torture, but it had ultimately saved him. She had hung around the docks when he and Patrick went out sailing, temptation personified. She and her friends sat in the bleachers at the ball field, laughing, joking, flirting and taunting him as he covered third base for his team. Evan had learned to fight the regular flashes of lust he had for Anna Berzani—fight them and *win*. He was not getting involved with her, not then and not now.

Even at sixteen, Anna might as well have had *forever* tattooed across her forehead. She was and always would be a Berzani. And the Berzanis were about family and all it entailed: a house, two cars in the driveway, a swing set in the backyard and a horde of kids running everywhere. All the obligations made Evan shudder and break out in a cold sweat.

He wondered, not for the first time, why she fought her connection with that tradition. The Berzanis were saints compared to his folks. When he was twelve years old, he had found sanctuary in her lively, loving family. That summer, he and Patrick had forged an unbreakable bond over their love of sailing and boats. When school began again and his parents' marriage started imploding, Evan had been practically adopted by Elaine and Antonio Berzani. They had given him respite from the battles in his own house, battles waged over money, love and a child's loyalty to each of his demanding parents. He loved being a part of the Berzani clan, but when she turned eighteen, Anna couldn't leave them fast enough. Why? What was she running from?

If Anna had any weakness, it was her relationship with her family. That's where he should attack, Evan realized. The love-hate relationship she had with her parents as a teenager hadn't changed much. He could use that to his advantage, convince her that they had a problem only she could solve. No matter how much noise she made to the contrary, she could not refuse to help them. He grinned and slapped the railing: she was as good as hooked.

Evan turned away from the water and walked back across the street. Stopping at one of the stands set up on the Justin Herman Plaza, he surveyed the bouquets arranged by a florist to tempt passersby. He reached for a bunch of flaming orange roses that reminded him of Anna's fiery red hair. He put them to his nose. The petals against his lips felt as soft as her skin had when he had kissed her cheek.

He paid the exorbitant price for the bouquet and returned to his hotel. Armed with her address and flowers to soften her heart, all he needed now was a favorable field of conquest. He would take her out to dinner, at the restaurant of her choosing. A little wine, good food and intimate conversation: Evan imagined the scene. She wouldn't be able to resist the full force of his charm, especially when he was pleading on her family's behalf.

And if she proved unassailable? He would just have to pull out all the stops. The possibilities sent a shiver over his skin and he pushed the thought away. Some methods were off-limits, no matter how worthy the prize and tantalizing the victim.

Chapter Two

Anna closed the door to her condo behind her. She dropped her purse and keys on a small table just inside the entry, then sifted through the mail she had collected from her mailbox. Nothing was of interest: bills, statements, junk mail. She tapped the envelopes back into a pile and tossed them beside her keys. Kicking off her shoes, she walked to the kitchen. The polished oak floors cooled her tired feet. Twelve hours in high heels was too much. There ought to be a law against that kind of torture.

Slipping off her suit jacket, she draped it over a chair, pulled open the refrigerator door and grabbed an open bottle of wine out of the rack. There was just about one serving remaining; exactly what she needed to recuperate from the day.

The chardonnay was cold and tart, with just a hint of sweetness. She sipped and walked back into the living room, tugging on the hem of her blouse as she went, freeing it from the waistband of her skirt. Sitting on the red leather sofa that faced a wide wall of windows, Anna put her feet up on the coffee table. She sipped the wine again, then rested the stem of the glass on her stomach. A small sigh escaped as she leaned her head back and closed her eyes: peace, at last.

While it hadn't been the day from hell, it had scorched

her enough. Evan McKenzie had disrupted everything. Sarah had twittered around the office like a drunken canary, rhapsodizing over his handsome charm. Anna was *more* rattled, not less, after yelling at Patrick. She had been unable to concentrate in her meetings or on her design work. Finally, she had closed herself in her office and brooded, wondering about Evan's motives and what he would do next.

Anna lifted her head and took another drink of wine, frowning when the door buzzer sounded. Since it wasn't the intercom in the lobby, she assumed it was one of her neighbors at the door, probably Jill from the fourth floor wanting to go out for sushi. Anna wasn't up for the latest installment of "Pigs I Have Slept With." She liked the woman in small doses, but her dating life was a running promotion for celibacy. Anna took another sip and ignored the summons. She groaned when it buzzed again, more insistently. Setting her glass on an end table, she went to the door. Hand on the doorknob, she peered through the peephole. Her heart nearly stopped.

Not again.

She turned and leaned back against the cold metal panel, as if to prevent it from flying open. There was no way she was opening this door. Hadn't she gotten rid of him once today? What sins had she committed to deserve this? She pretended she wasn't home, but the door buzzer seemed to know better. It sounded again. This time it didn't end. Droning on and on, the noise grated on her nerves like fingernails on a chalkboard. Finally, Anna spun around and wrenched open the door.

"Stop pestering me!"

"Whoa! Easy there, girl. A bit high-strung, are we?" Evan McKenzie asked with a grin. His gaze slid over her. "And my, aren't you looking lovely tonight."

Shoeless, shirttail flapping, looking as tired as she felt, Anna knew otherwise. She glared at him. "How did you get in here? As I remember, there's a security system in the lobby."

"A very nice woman let me in as she left. Tall with blond hair?"

Jill. Anna steamed. Of course she would have granted Evan whatever he asked for—just like every other woman in the world. Well, Anna wasn't going to run in that particular stampede. "What do you want now?"

"To take you to dinner of course."

"I'm not hungry. Go away." She started to close the door, but he stepped forward, stopping her.

"Take pity on this poor stranger, a lost soul left to wander aimlessly in your fair city," he said. His face was serious now, long lashes screening the expression in his eyes. "You're my only hope for a dinner companion."

"Go find Jill, the woman who let you in. Unit 408. She prefers sushi."

"She's no substitute for you. Come on, Annie," he added, his voice low and coaxing. "For old time's sake."

Anna wanted to growl. She did *not* want to go out to dinner with Evan. The more she saw of him, the more aggravated she would become. Before she could answer, he produced a bunch of roses from behind his back. They were a bright flame in the dim light of the hall. Anna couldn't help reaching out to take them.

"They're lovely." She buried her nose in the blossoms and breathed in their heady sweetness. Irritated with her own weakness, she held the roses at arm's length, trying to give them back to Evan. He put his hands in his pockets, foiling her efforts. "I'm sure they would impress Jill."

"Probably, but they're for you."

"Why are you bombarding me with heavy artillery?"

"Because I'm hungry and want to take you to dinner." A sly smile tilted one corner of Evan's mouth. "Your mother's going to be *very* disappointed when I tell her you wouldn't even have dinner with me."

The ridiculous threat brought a reluctant smile to Anna's lips, then she sighed, knowing she had been beaten. She stepped aside, motioning him to enter. "Come in. I have to change."

"Not on my account."

"No, on mine," she said sourly. There was no way she was going out in public looking like she did. For one, she needed the armor that only good attire could provide. And, though he had changed clothes, Evan still looked like a fashion model. His charcoal wool suit fit so well, it had to be custom-made. His tie was green this time, echoing the color of his eyes and intensifying their pull.

"Have a seat. Do you want something to drink?" she asked.

"No, I'm fine." He walked a few steps into the room and stopped as Anna closed the door. "So, this is your secret lair."

Anna refused to rise to that bait. She went to the kitchen and brought a tall glass vase out of a cupboard and filled it with a little water. Peeling the tissue paper away from the stems and clipping the rubber bands that secured them, she arranged the roses in the vase. As she worked, she watched Evan from the corner of her eye. He walked to the middle of the room and turned a slow circle.

"No wonder your parents can't pry you out of San Francisco," he remarked.

Anna smiled as she poured more water into the vase, feeling a flush of pleasure at the implied compliment. She loved her high-ceilinged, airy condo. And she did think of it as her lair, her hideaway. A former sugar warehouse,

the oak floors showed the scars and stains from the pallets
and crates of raw sugar that had been slid across them.
Overhead, the ceiling was crisscrossed with ducts and an
exposed sprinkler system, all painted navy blue. The walls
were exposed brick with plaster still clinging in rough,
ragged sections—except for the front wall. That was en-
tirely windows, floor to ceiling. Long drapes which could
be drawn over them framed the view, but Anna seldom
bothered to close them. With the panorama of the Bay,
there was no one outside who could easily see into her
home. The seagulls didn't seem interested in whatever they
saw.

Evan prowled across the hardwood floor, stopping in
front of three paintings hanging on the far wall.

"Is this Tangier Island?" he asked, looking away from
the middle canvas.

"Mmm. And that one's up the Sassafras River. The other
is the entrance to Queenstown Creek."

"Can't take the Chesapeake out of the girl, can you?"

"It's always good to remember where you come from."
She shrugged. "Make yourself at home. I won't be long."

"Take your time." Evan had wandered over to the bookcase and pulled out a volume on French architecture as she
escaped into her bedroom.

Anna sat on the bed for a moment and closed her eyes.
Drawing a deep breath into her lungs, she held it, then let
it out slowly. *It's just dinner with a family friend.* He would
be gone tomorrow. Rising, she went to the closet and pulled
out a dress. Surveying her random pick, she decided it
was perfect for this nondate date. A golden-tan silk, it was
slim-fitting, but sedate, sleeveless with a slightly scooped
neckline. The skirt ended just above her knees, flaring out
at the bottom in a series of pleats.

She quickly changed, then fixed her makeup before

brushing her hair. The bright red curls bounced as she ran her fingers through to settle them into submission. Looking at herself in the mirror, she wondered if Evan would see the edgy nerves that she saw lurking in her dark brown eyes. *Not if you don't let him.* She turned away and slipped on shoes, then picked up a pair of earrings and carried them with her to the living room.

Evan was standing with his back to her, staring out the window. As she came to his side, she noticed that he had her glass in one hand. "Excellent wine," he said, raising it to her, then taking a sip. "Nice view, too."

"I believe you complimented me on that earlier today. You're repeating yourself already and we've been together less than an hour," she said.

He turned and gazed first at her hair, then at the topaz earrings she slipped into place. "Just because it's repeated, doesn't mean it can't be true twice. But the first view is better than the second."

Anna shook her head. "Men."

Evan shrugged, his eyes unrepentant. "Ready?"

"Yes." She turned and walked over to the table that held her purse. "And starving, too."

"You recover your appetite quick. And your good looks," Evan said, setting the wineglass on the table as he followed her. "The third view is the best of all."

She hoped he didn't see the flush that crept up her cheeks. His opinion didn't matter. Not anymore. "Thanks, but flattery will get you nowhere."

Evan laughed. "Are you kidding? It gets *me* everywhere."

She shot him a glance, then picked up her keys and put them in her purse.

"What?" he asked. "You think I have hidden motives?"

"That goes without saying." Grabbing a light gray poplin coat from the closet, she motioned to the door. But before she could move forward, Evan took her coat from her and held it open. For a second as she put it on, she was close to him and could smell the tang of his aftershave again. She swallowed and pulled away, belting the garment around her waist.

"Such a gentleman." She kept her tone faintly mocking. "Trying to impress me, McKenzie?"

"You, Berzani? Why bother?" he asked with a scoff. "I know better than that."

Anna pursed her lips, opened the door and led the way out of her apartment.

"We can get a taxi on Market. It's just a couple of blocks," she said as they exited the lobby.

As they rounded the corner, Evan pointed to the cable car that was slowly revolving around on a huge turntable. "What about riding on that?"

"Are you kidding? Nobody takes them."

"Really," he said. One eyebrow rose as he surveyed the queue waiting to board. "Somebody better tell all those poor ignorant people."

Anna had to laugh. She made a show of looking around for eavesdroppers, then said in a low voice, "Those are tourists. Don't tell them, but no one *from* here takes cable cars unless we have out-of-town visitors. It's against the rules." She raised a hand and a taxi slid to the curb next to them. "California and Grant, please," she told the driver.

Minutes later, they arrived at the ornate Dragon's Gate that marked the southern edge of Chinatown. The gate was shadowed, as the sun set behind the buildings, but numerous shop signs backlit the golden dragons raging across the top. On the gate's green-tile roof, large fish leaped in the last rays of the sun, while smaller carvings in front swam in darkness. The passage was teeming with people of every ethnicity, jostling one another as they entered and exited Chinatown.

Anna dived in and up the steps through the gate, weaving expertly through the throng. Evan followed, grabbing her arm.

"Slow down, Annie. Did I miss the starting gun?"

"Sorry. I'm just used to walking here alone."

"What, you don't get any hot dates for pot stickers and fried rice?" he asked as he took her hand and tucked it into the crook of his arm. She tugged away, but he put his hand over hers and smiled down at her. "Don't be difficult. I can't afford to lose you in this crowd. You're shorter than most of the natives."

"I am not," she said testily.

He merely grinned at her without comment. She glared up at him, then turned and led him along Grant Street. As they walked, he slowed occasionally and took in the chaos of the shops that lined the streets. Tables of porcelain figurines, brass incense burners, paper fans and numerous curios spilled out of many shop doors. The windows above the tables were crowded with all kinds of goods for sale, from bamboo steamers to paintings of cherry blossoms on silk.

"Is it always this busy?" he asked.

"No. Sometimes it's worse." Anna dodged a man and a woman hunched over a display of wooden Buddhas. "Weekends are the craziest, especially on the tourist streets. I usually come over on Saturdays and do my shopping on the side streets. The vegetable vendors have some incredible stuff."

As they made their way up the sidewalk, Anna tried not to enjoy getting jostled against Evan. The same mix of exhilaration and irritation that had plagued her earlier returned. She told herself it was natural. He was an attractive man and she wasn't immune to his charms. More than one woman had turned to stare at Evan. One went so far as to deliberately step into his path, feigning an accidental collision, hoping to catch him with her beguiling smile. The fact that he was with another woman meant nothing to her. She was simply a moth to his flame.

When Evan returned her daring look with nothing more than a nod, Anna was surprised. For a moment, she felt a rush of satisfaction. Had he ignored the other women simply because he was with *her?* The feeling was quickly smothered when she concluded that Evan was ignoring her, too. He was completely taken by the seductive bustle and chaos of Chinatown.

Anna grit her teeth and told herself it didn't matter. This was not a date. But she couldn't help the words that popped out of her mouth. "She looked like your girlfriend. What's her name again? Dippy?"

Evan scowled. "*Kippy.* And she's not my girlfriend anymore."

"Oh? Too bad," Anna said casually, though her pulse had picked up pace at this news.

"Not really. Why limit myself to one fish, when there's a whole ocean," Evan said with a grin and a wink. Then his focus shifted and he stopped at a display of good-luck charms, a bowl filled with flat, polished rocks etched with Chinese characters. "What do you suppose these say?"

Anna smiled wryly to herself, even while her heart felt a pang of sadness. If she wanted proof of her folly in being attracted to Evan, here it was in plain English: no one woman would *ever* be special to this man. She pushed her foolish fantasies to the back of her mind and answered him in an even tone, "Probably 'long life,' 'wisdom,' 'lots of luck,' that sort of thing."

"Right." Evan snorted. He looked over at Anna, his green eyes dancing with amusement. "I bet they say 'Eat at Chan's' or 'Go Home Stupid Tourist.'"

Anna had to laugh. "The English-speaking world may never know the truth."

"Hey, how about that place?" Evan said, pointing to a restaurant with a line out the door. "It was recommended by the hotel."

"Too busy and too touristy." Anna shook her head and kept moving up the street. "The Pan-king has good food, but it's always packed. I know another place up a few blocks and off the main drag. It's the real thing. Trust me."

"You're a genuine San Franciscan, aren't you?"

"And proud of it."

"No regrets about leaving family so far away?"

"Nope. We like each other better from a distance."

"They miss you, you know."

"Don't start, Evan," she said with a sigh. Anna felt a pang as she spoke, but shook it off. They walked in silence for a while. She was grateful to see the sign for the restaurant loom brightly in the darkness. "We're here."

They stood at the top of stairs that descended into the basement of a three-story building. The sign of lit red Chinese characters was the only indication that the place was actually open—or that there might be a business here at all.

"Are you sure about this place?" Evan whispered as he followed her down the steps.

"Trust me," she repeated.

"It's the restaurant I don't trust. Does the health department even know it's down here?"

She laughed. "I never knew you were so persnickety about food." Anna pushed through a door into a dimly lit entrance with dark red walls and black trim.

"I just like to know what I'm eating."

A short, middle-aged, stoic-faced hostess appeared from behind a screen. "Two?"

"Please," Anna said.

The woman picked up menus and motioned them to follow. She escorted them to a booth on one side of the dining room. Many of the other tables were full. Several of the large, round ones held what looked like extended families, from swaddled babies to ancient grandparents. A mixture of chattered languages filled the room. At the table, Evan helped Anna slip off her coat, then slid into the booth opposite her.

When they were seated, the hostess gave them the menus, bowed and left them alone. Seconds later, a young man in an apron brought a white teapot to the table. He turned their cups over, poured tea into both, then set the pot on the table between them. Scooping up the extra two place settings, he left without uttering a word.

"What's the name of this hidden establishment?" Evan asked.

"Actually, I don't know. I don't read Chinese." When Evan looked doubtfully at her, Anna shrugged and picked up the menu. "So what looks good to you?"

"Your guess is better than mine. I can't read Chinese, either," Evan said, putting his menu aside and sipping the small cup of tea. "I'll eat anything that isn't wiggling."

"Okay, that leaves out the dancing shrimp."

"*Live* shrimp?" Evan grimaced. "And I thought I was only joking."

"You have to be careful what you order. Just about anything goes," Anna said with a grin. "They don't serve them here, but I know a place that does. They're brought in a bowl and you pull the heads off, peel and eat them on the spot."

"Okay, maybe not." He obviously found the idea revolting.

"What? You eat raw oysters, don't you?"

"Sometimes. That's different."

"How so?" She cocked her head to one side, pursing her lips skeptically.

"Oysters don't *dance*."

"If they could, I bet they would." Anna leaned forward, unable to stop herself from torturing him. "Doing the foxtrot all the way down your throat."

Evan stared at her in surprise, then laughed. "You *still* have an overactive imagination. San Francisco hasn't changed that."

Anna laughed, too, then perused the menu in front of her, reading the convenient English translation for each dish. Usually their banter was more savage, cutting even, but tonight it seemed that each had retracted the claws and fangs. She felt flushed. This evening was turning out far differently than she had expected. Despite her earlier admonishments to herself, she couldn't deny herself the tantalizing pleasure of enjoying Evan's company.

"I'll pick the wine. You choose the *well-cooked* delicacies," he said, his green eyes pinning her with a mock-stern stare.

"Coward. Where's your spirit of adventure?"

"It stops shy of food that's trying to escape," he said, scrutinizing the wine selections. "White?"

"As long as it's dry."

The waiter arrived at that moment. "Good evening. Something to drink?" His voice was thickly accented, but quite precise, with a touch of British Hong Kong.

"A bottle of your Luna Napa pinot grigio, please," Evan said.

"Okay," the waiter said, scratching on his pad. "You want appetizer?"

"We'll have the shrimp pot stickers," Anna said, flashing a glance at Evan. "And the tofu with cilantro, please."

"Bok choy with spicy radish pickle is very good. Fresh tonight."

"We'll have that, too," Evan said. As the waiter scribbled furiously on his pad then hurried off to the kitchen, Evan added, "There's no such thing as too much Chinese food."

"Fine by me. Whatever we don't eat will be my lunch tomorrow." Anna pulled the chopsticks and fork out of her folded napkin, then spread the cloth over her lap. Evan followed suit.

"How in the world did you find this place?" he asked.

Anna shrugged. "Like I find all the best spots in Chinatown. I was wandering around with a friend and we saw several people going down the stairs and decided to try it."

The waiter appeared with a wine bottle, showed it to them, expertly uncorked it and filled both their glasses. Evan picked his up and toasted Anna. "To new adventures."

"I'm not sure I want to toast that," Anna said with a frown.

He reached over and tapped his glass against hers anyway. "Sure you do."

She sipped her wine, watching him warily. Lowering her glass to the table, she said, "Sorry, Evan. My answer is still no. I already told Patrick that, too."

Evan leaned forward, his elbows on the table. His lips tilted in a slight smile, obviously amused by her bluntness. "Come on, don't you want to help your poor old parents? They really need it."

Anna had to laugh at his wheedling tone. "You are such a pain in the ass, you know that?"

"Yes, but a charming one," he said, eyes laughing at her over the rim of his glass as he took a drink.

"More persistent than charming," Anna countered drily. "Level with me, Evan. What's in this for you?"

"For one, I expect to get a healthy return on the money and time I put into the deal. But I'm mostly doing it for your folks. They've done a lot for me. And it makes sense for them."

Anna frowned and looked away for a moment. "You know, you don't need *me* to design anything. Any local architect can do the job."

Evan returned his glass to the table and twisted the stem back and forth, his gaze on the tawny liquid inside. He narrowed his eyes a little when he looked up at her. "Maybe," he conceded, "but you're the one we want. Look, your parents built A&E Marine from virtually nothing. For twenty-two years, they poured their blood and sweat into that boatyard."

"I know the story, Evan." Anna sighed impatiently. "I've heard it a thousand times. I *lived* it, for—"

"Wait a minute and hear me out, Annie," he said. "The only thing on this earth more important to Antonio and Elaine Berzani than that business is their children and grandchildren. Family is everything to them. You know that. Like it or not, that includes you. Why do you think they meddle in your life all the time?"

"To drive me slowly insane?" Anna muttered.

Evan ignored her and continued, "Because your happiness matters to them. And because they want—they *expect*—to participate in their children's lives. Just as they expect their children to participate in theirs."

"I let my mother set me up on blind dates, don't I?"

"And bitch every minute, too. But that's not my point."

"So, what *is* the point, then?"

"They need more from you now, Anna. From all their children. It's time for A&E Marine to change, and though he realizes the truth of that, it's still going to be hard for your dad. Your mom's having trouble with it, too. It hurts because the reality they're having to face is that they are getting old and no one wants to take over the boatyard as it stands. Not Patrick and not Ian, even though they've been running it for the past few years. They both have other plans for their lives. You and Jeannie certainly don't want to take over. If we don't do something now, it will die a slow, sad death while everyone wrangles about who's going to take responsibility. So, to survive, it has to change. To change, your parents need to let go. That's only going to happen if their children help make the transition." Evan speared her with a sharp look, his expression as serious as she had ever seen it. "*All* of their children."

Anna sighed and took a healthy drink from her glass.

"Bottom line," Evan added. "Patrick and I think your parents won't cooperate with any other architect but you."

Anna set her glass down, avoiding looking at him. She toyed with her chopsticks, waiting for him to go on, but he was silent. Finally, she glanced up and met his gaze. "How long have you worked on this speech? It's very good."

"It's also very true."

"You make it tough to say no." She glared at him, but he simply looked back at her.

"I want to make it impossible. Let me add that you, more than any other architect, can put the family stamp on a design. You could make sure the Berzani character and tradition is preserved in whatever we build. That would mean a lot to your dad. To your mom, too."

"*Any* good architect can do that."

"I doubt it. They're certainly not going to do it as well as you can. Besides, your parents trust *you* more than they'd trust some stranger."

"They can learn to trust someone else," she said with an exasperated huff.

"Not likely."

The waiter brought their appetizers and set them on the table before Evan could speak. When the man asked for their dinner order, Anna gave it: shrimp egg-foo-yung, deep-fried catfish, Chinese vegetables and spicy Hunan pork. When he was gone, she scooped up two of the pot stickers and handed the plate to Evan. Between them they divided the food.

"You're going to say yes, Annie. Why not just get it over with?" Evan asked as he sliced a pot sticker in two. He looked over at her, his eyes dancing with humor. "By the way, I packed a tent and a sleeping bag. I'm camping out in your lobby and badgering you until you do."

She didn't want to be charmed, but she had to admit he was getting to her. Not that she would ever admit it. Picking up a piece of tofu with her chopsticks, Anna popped it into her mouth. It had a fresh, slightly bitter flavor. When she had chewed and swallowed, she said with a slight smile, "Trust me, you haven't said anything new that would change my mind. Why don't you just let me enjoy my meal?"

"We'd both enjoy it more if you just admitted I'm right, Annie Berzani." His face was earnest, his tone chirping, a perfect imitation of Anna's mother.

Anna stared at him, then lowered her chopsticks to the table and laughed loudly. "It's scary how good you are at that."

Evan grinned. Anna shook her head and dabbed tears of laughter from the corners of her eyes with her napkin. Still chuckling, she took up her chopsticks again and they ate in silence for a while.

Drizzling soy sauce on her plate and dipping a piece of pickled radish in it, she asked, "You know if I say yes, it will be all the encouragement my dad needs."

"What do you mean? Encouragement?" Evan raised an eyebrow as he ate a bite of tofu.

"He'll take it as a sign that I've finally come to my senses and returned to the family fold."

Evan chuckled. "I suppose you have a point there."

"I can just hear him." Anna sat back and took a drink of wine. She lowered her voice and added a slight accent as she said, *"I knew you would see sense, Anna Maria. Now you can give me many grandchildren to keep me happy for my last years."*

"First you'd have to have a husband," Evan said drily.

"Oh, God," Anna moaned, closing her eyes. "Ma will be beside herself, too. I'll have to go on more of those awful dates she sets up."

"I don't know, I kind of liked the accountant she fixed you up with last time."

Anna glared at him, remembering when Evan had happened to be at the bar where she was meeting one of her mother's first-round picks. His teasing had been particularly merciless, not helping the nausea she had felt. Dating a man preapproved by her mother had been horrible enough. Anna pointed her chopsticks at Evan. "I was so mad at you. You should have disappeared as soon as he showed up."

"Are you kidding?" Evan chortled. "Watching you turn that shade of green was priceless. Besides, you should thank me. I got rid of him for you, didn't I?"

"That poor man," she said, slowly shaking her head.

She smiled, then giggled, unable to hold on to her anger. What a farce, at least when she saw it from a distance. "He didn't know what to do when you sat down and bought him a drink."

"Elaine gave me hell about it later, if that's any comfort."

"She thought the guy was perfect for me." Anna shuddered. "Not in this lifetime."

The waiter arrived back at the table, cleared the appetizers and set the main course between them. Steam wafted upward from the plates, bearing amazing scents. Evan picked up the dish nearest to him and handed it to her.

"This looks weird, but smells delicious," he said as he lifted another plate.

They filled their plates and began to eat. The catfish was crisp in its light batter coating, nearly melting on her tongue. The vegetables were perfectly cooked and the spicy pork burst with flavor in her mouth.

"So, about the project—"

"No!" Anna held up a hand in protest. "No more until *after* dinner. Give me a chance to enjoy and digest."

"But the only chance I get to speak uninterrupted is when you have food in your mouth," Evan teased.

Anna decided to retaliate. "Let's change the topic a bit. How's your mother and hubby number four?"

"Number six, actually."

Anna nearly choked on the bite of rice she had just popped in her mouth. She swallowed, sipped her tea and stared at him. "Six? Why so many?"

"Eventually they all get tired of ducking the same pots and pans she threw at Dad."

"Wow." Anna looked over at Evan, at a loss for words. She realized she had never really heard him talk about his parents' divorce. Though his tone was matter-of-fact, she wondered if he was as blasé as he sounded. "I never knew it was that bad."

He caught her sympathetic look and smiled slightly. "Don't get upset, Annie. It was a long time ago. My mom's just never been able to move on."

"Is she happy with this one?" she asked, leaning forward.

"For now, I suppose. With her batting average, I figure she's got another six months." Evan was quiet for a minute, then shrugged. "She'd be happier if she were single, but she never listens to my advice."

"In my experience, parents never listen to their children," Anna said, sitting back again, thinking of her own mother and father.

"She has this crazy idea that she needs to be married. You'd think marriage to my dad would have cured her." Evan shook his head. "It cured him, anyway."

"He's never remarried?"

"No. And he's happier than she is. So what does that tell you?"

"That your parents are screwed up. That's all. You should look at examples of normal couples."

Evan dished up more vegetables and pork. He glanced at Anna. "The only happy marriage I know is your parents'. So, between mine and yours, that's seven-to-one against. Not good odds."

"Not fair. Your mother skews the data."

"Or does she confirm it?" he asked with a wink.

Anna laughed a bit helplessly. "What about Patrick and Kate, or Ian and Mimi?" Both her older brothers had married recently and were giddily content.

"Too soon to tell. Both relationships could fall apart tomorrow."

"I can understand why you're such a cynic, but Charlie and Jeannie are happy and that's been nearly fourteen years," she said, referring to her eldest sister.

"Another fluke." He smiled, but it didn't quite reach his eyes. Lurking in the depths she thought she saw a touch of grim mockery. "Besides, they're all Berzanis. I'm a McKenzie."

"So?"

"It's like comparing apples and pineapples. Maybe Berzanis stick to their spouses, but McKenzies don't. That's been proven."

"Only by your parents. That has nothing to do with you."

Evan laughed, but there wasn't much humor in the sound. "I'm my father's son, Annie. No denying that."

Anna held his gaze, disquieted by his fatalism, yet not sure if he was serious. She looked down to her plate again, confusion sweeping through her. So what if Even McKenzie disdained marriage? That meant nothing to her. Unless... Anna stopped herself from finishing the thought. She was not going there. She knew a dangerous path when she saw one, and that one had red warning signs and flashing yellow lights posted all over it.

PUSHING BACK HIS PLATE, Evan sighed. "Kudos on your choice. That was fantastic. The best Chinese food I've ever had."

Anna smiled. She had quit eating long before Evan had finished, watching with ill-concealed amazement as he had first one, then a second helping of everything. "You ate like a pig. There's nothing left for my lunch."

"The way you eat, there's plenty," he said, surveying the remains. "Here, have some more pork."

Anna shook her head. "You're just like my father. He's always trying to stuff me with pasta."

"I'll take that as a compliment. And speaking of your father—"

The waiter arrived, interrupting him. "You want a box?"

"Yes, thanks," Anna said, grateful for the diversion.

They sat back as the waiter removed the plates. When he had gone, Evan poured the rest of the wine out. He opened his mouth to speak, but Anna beat him to it.

"My answer is still no," she said softly. "Sorry. You'll have to find someone else."

Evan looked at her intently. She smiled, but her dark eyes were serious. He sighed and took a drink of his wine. "At least tell me you'll think about it."

She inclined her head. "Sure."

"Liar," he said sourly.

She laughed and he was enchanted once again, just as he had been over and over tonight. Evan gripped tight the reins of his attraction to her. But even now, hearing her laugh, looking into her eyes, he could feel his control slipping. This entire evening had been a wonder and a curse. His strategy of taking her to dinner and charming her had backfired. *He* was the one charmed—dangerously so.

From the moment she opened the door to her condo, he had had a hard time reminding himself that this was business. She had looked delightfully disheveled in her stocking feet, hair curling around her face. Hard to resist. No less so when she came out wearing this dress. The simple, unadorned silk molded to her hips and breasts. The heels she wore drew attention to her sleek legs and delicate ankles. He was burned by the loveliness of her fiery hair, highlighted by the gold tone of the fabric. She was more beautiful than he remembered.

It hadn't gotten any easier since then. Talking with her, sparring with her, only added to his attraction. In their typical encounters they sniped at each other like the teenagers they once were. Sometimes, they just glared at each other. Tonight there had been a shift, a playfulness to their exchanges that had unsettled Evan. He admitted to himself that he was fighting hard to keep the distance between them. *Just a while longer,* he warned himself. *Keep it together, McKenzie.*

The waiter returned with a plastic bag full of small boxes and asked if they wanted any dessert. They both declined and he put a tray with the bill and two fortune cookies on the table between them. Evan plucked the receipt from the tray just as Anna reached for it.

"You're not buying," she said, trying to snatch the bill away from him.

"Yes, I am," Evan countered. He slipped a hand into his jacket and drew out his wallet. Pulling out a credit card, he handed it, and the bill, to the man.

"One moment," the waiter said with a slight bow, retreating from the table.

"You don't have to buy me dinner," Anna said, "especially since I refused your request."

"My treat. And my write-off," he added with a grin, deliberately reminding himself and her that they were here to discuss business. Picking up the cookies from the tray, he tossed one to Anna, then snapped open the other. He read the slip of paper with a grimace. "'Your lover will never wish to leave you.' That's not a fortune, that's a threat. What's yours say?"

Anna broke open her cookie. "This is probably yours," she said, handing him the paper.

"'Fortune smiles on the bold,'" he read and laughed. "Definitely more to my liking. I must have picked up your cookie." He nudged the paper he had dropped to the table along with the broken cookie. A disturbing thought struck him. Narrowing his eyes, he forced himself to lean back in his seat. "So, who's this lover that's not going to leave you?"

When Anna blushed, her fair skin turning a becoming rose, Evan felt himself tense.

"None of your business," she said crisply.

"So there is someone. Who is he?" he pressed.

"Evan. Let it go." Her tone was exasperated, but the blush still colored her cheeks, and she wasn't meeting his eyes. "There's no one."

"I don't believe you." He didn't, either. She was too attractive to *not* have men hanging around. Evan found himself ready to demand an answer. As if the truth would set him free, he thought wryly. Maybe it was better not to know.

"You don't have to believe me," Anna said, taking a bite of her cookie.

"A secret lover? Is he married?"

She shook her head.

"Come on, Annie," Evan said, forcing a brief laugh. "Your mother is going to grill me about you when I get back. You've got to give me something to feed her."

"Satisfying my mother is not my job," Anna countered. "Debriefing her is not in your job description, either."

"It's easier to give her something than have her nag me."

"Tell her I'm busy, happy and healthy."

"And dating?"

"No one special," she said with a shake of her head.

Something like a rubber band snapped inside Evan, leaving him a bit light-headed. He drew in a deep breath and tried to find his footing again. "She won't be happy with that news."

"Life is filled with little disappointments."

"You've proved that to me over and over today," he said as the waiter slipped a credit-card receipt in front of him and offered a pen. Evan added a tip and signed the paper in a scrawl. Handing one copy back to the other man, he smiled. "Thanks."

The waiter nodded solemnly and disappeared. Anna slid out of the booth and picked up her purse as Evan took her coat and helped her into it, settling the fabric around her shoulders. Soft strands of her hair tickled his hands, tempting him to sift through it. Not for the first time, he measured himself against her height. Small and slight, she would fit just under his chin. He stepped back and motioned her to lead the way out of the restaurant.

On the street again, they turned toward the main gate. The crowds had thinned to a few couples strolling along the sidewalk. Most of the shops were closed and barred for the night. Evan didn't tuck Anna's hand into the crook of his arm again. Touching her would be a mistake. Instead, he stuck his hands in his pockets and walked silently at her side.

"Oh! I forgot the food," Anna said with a start.

"Do you want to go back?"

"No. It's not important."

"But you'll starve tomorrow."

"In this town?" Anna asked with a laugh. "Not likely."

They walked on and Evan sensed the evening coming to a close—too soon for him, he realized. He reminded himself of the mess his parents had made of their lives—and his childhood. Evan knew he was too much like his father, too needful of his freedom and his space to endure in a marriage. Whatever attraction had sparked between him and Anna, he must extinguish it soon or repeat the same mistake.

When they reached the Dragon's Gate, a taxi was just disgorging its passengers. Evan grabbed the door and held it while Anna slipped inside. The taxi pulled away from the curb as Anna gave the driver her address. This was a night out of time, that's how he had to see it, just a few fleeting hours of magic that would soon be over and must never return to earth again.

Chapter Three

"Do you want to be dropped at your hotel?" Anna glanced over at Evan, his face a silhouette in the dimness.

"No. I'll see you home first, then walk back from there."

"You don't have to do that."

"I never do anything I don't have to, Annie," he said, a thread of humor lacing through his words.

Outside her building, Evan paid the driver and helped Anna out of the cab. He cupped her elbow and ushered her into the building before she could wish him good-night, then followed her through the lobby and to the elevator without a word. At her door, she unlocked and pushed it open. Stepping inside, she flipped a switch and soft light shone from a few spots on the ceiling. Evan followed her, closing the door behind him, but he didn't venture far into the room.

"Do you want something to drink?" she asked, but he was already shaking his head.

"I'd better go. I've got an early flight."

There was an awkward pause—awkward for Anna at least. This was the moment the girl was supposed to wait for the guy to kiss her. Her heart sped at the thought, but she chided herself. *Get a grip. This is not a date.* She set her purse and keys on the table by the door. Swallowing to clear her dry throat, she sought the words to end this odd, enchanting evening.

"Thanks for the roses, dinner and, uh, everything," she finished lamely and looked down, hoping the shadows and dim lighting hid her embarrassment. Forcing a self-conscious smile to her lips, she took a step toward him. Rising up on tiptoe, she put one hand on his shoulder for balance and pressed a quick, sisterly kiss to his cheek. Her lips tingled from the contact with his skin, slightly bristled and warm.

Evan jerked and his hands came to her waist in a hard grip. Still on her toes, Anna was caught off balance, her other hand coming up to rest on his chest. His jacket was open and her fingers splayed against the crisp cotton of his shirt, pushing his tie aside. She could feel the warmth of his skin, the tantalizing roughness of the curling hair under the fabric.

His scent filled her head and she swayed toward him. When his lips brushed against hers she froze for an instant, her eyelids sliding closed. The delicate touch was a lick of fire from her head to her toes. She had wanted this for so long; it was just as potent as she had dreamed. Evan drew away and Anna couldn't stop the whimper of longing that came from her throat, nearly soundless above the pounding of her heart. It wasn't enough. She wanted—she *needed*—more. Opening her eyes, she focused on the seductive curve of his mouth, aching for the promise behind the tease of his kiss.

"Good night, Annie," Evan said softly, the words a whisper. His expression was calm, cold even. "And goodbye."

Anna stiffened and a blush, deeper than before, suffused her cheeks. He was obviously immune to the power of their kiss. Pulling away from his touch, Anna looked down again, knowing she had let herself be swept away.

She had misled herself. Closing her eyes tightly, she groped for balance. How could she have been so foolish? Evan was still Evan.

She was startled when his hands came up on either side of her head. Her gaze flew up to meet his at the first touch of his fingers in her hair. Fingertips stroking her neck through the curls, his thumbs touched her cheeks and lifted her face to his.

"What's wrong?" he asked. His voice was low and intimate, sending a shiver of fear and need down her spine.

Anna could only look up at him, mute with humiliation. Evan's eyes narrowed as her teeth worried her lower lip. For an instant, the spark of heat in the green depths took her breath away. There and gone so quickly, she wondered if she had imagined it. Seconds later, as if to answer her thought, his lips met hers again—warm, firm and certain.

She lost her grip. She was drowning in the kiss. There was nowhere to go but down. The heat of his mouth, the strength of the arms that slipped around her, the pulse of the muscular body she pressed against, all swamped her senses. Her arms rose to encircle his neck in surrender, her hands pressed against the soft wool of his jacket. One of Evan's hands slid to her waist, pulling her up onto her toes again, into the curve of his body. The other fisted in her hair, holding her immobile. His kiss held an indefinable flavor she had craved for too long, a kiss so sweet and intoxicating, Anna only wanted more.

She sent a teasing foray into his mouth with her tongue. For one moment, his mated with hers in a hot slide of demand. Then he hesitated and pulled his lips from hers just the barest inch. They stayed that way for one moment and then another, the tension stretching unbearably. Evan's face was hard, his green eyes glittering, his jaw tensed. He looked like a man in pain and instinctively, Anna moved to soothe him. She closed the gap, touching her mouth to his, offering him anything he chose to take. In the next instant, Evan took command of the kiss. His mouth molded to hers, demanding a passion she was only too happy to give him.

Pushing her back against the wall, Evan's hands rushed over her. Anna's breath came in short gasps that had nothing to do with the weight of him and everything to do with the rough palms shaping her breasts, the hard fingers sliding her skirt up her thighs. He wanted her, just as much as she wanted him. All the years of suppressed passion rose to meet this hunger eagerly. It had been a mistake to think that she could resist it—*him*—now after so long. When he wrenched her coat over her shoulders, she responded by dragging at his suit jacket. A button popped to the floor as she fought clumsily to open his shirt.

All the fantasies she had ever had about this man came rushing in to swamp her senses and make them greedy for every touch, taste and torment: the warm skin under her palms, the sweet pressure of his lips on hers, the slow friction of his body to hers. Her heart felt light and, for a moment, she wanted to laugh. Why had she waited so long?

In seconds his shirt and tie were gone. She didn't know where they went or how they came off. She cared only that she had free rein of his hard, muscular chest. Her forays were interrupted when Evan unzipped the back of her dress and drew the fabric down, trapping her arms. He kissed his way down her throat to her breast, licking and biting gently as he went, turning her into a writhing bundle of need. Anna tried to wrest her hands free of her dress, but Evan held her captive.

Peeling back the lace of her bra, he took the tip of first one, then the other breast in his mouth. Anna's knees weakened as an arrow of pleasure darted right to her core. She forgot about freedom in the wash of heat that flushed her skin. When he pulled her dress down farther and pushed it to the floor, she let it slide away without thought.

"God, you are beautiful," he said in a rasp.

Evan's eyes, darkened to jade now, glowed as he watched his hand cup a breast, smooth his fingers down her stomach to toy with the lacy edge of her underwear. She had no compunction about standing in front of him dressed only in bra, panties and thigh-high stockings. Instead, she reveled in his obvious desire. She had wanted him to look at her—to *see* her—for so long. Finally, she had his undivided attention. The experience was far more glorious and wonderful than she had ever imagined.

At last, unable to stay quiescent any longer, she reached out and ran her palms up his arms. His eyes narrowed, hands sliding around her waist and stroking her back. Arms encircling his neck, Anna rose on tiptoe, pressing herself to him. The hard ridge of his erection throbbed against the juncture of her thighs, the wool of his trousers scratching her softer skin. Holding his eyes with hers, Anna swept her tongue over his lower lip in a soft, hot caress.

"Make love to me, Evan," she whispered against his mouth.

His arms slowly tightened around her, crushing her to his body. He deepened the kiss, sending her head spinning again. The dizziness intensified as she felt herself lifted up in his arms. Cradling her against his chest, Evan strode down the hall to her bedroom, leaving their clothes piled together on the wood floor.

Anna's heart beat with wild anticipation. There was no turning back now, for either of them. She was getting her wish. Finally, after all these years. Dreams did come true, she knew. You just had to wait for them—in this case, a very long time.

FIVE HOURS LATER, EVAN walked into his hotel room, stripped off his jacket and flung it across the room. Stalking to the window and the claustrophobic view of the office building across the street, he pressed the heels of his hands into the mullion. Leaning forward, he sucked in a deep breath before letting it out slowly.

What the hell had he done?

Staring out at the darkened offices, Evan's mind and body filled with Anna Berzani: her laughing eyes and soft, sweet lips; the silken swirl of her hair that begged to be touched; the slight, sleek length of her body that pressed so pliantly to his; the taste of her mouth and every satin inch of her skin. Closing his eyelids tightly, he tried to banish the sensations, but against his will, they only grew more palpable, more complete.

With a muffled growl, he pushed away from the window and went to the minibar. Grabbing one of the miniature bottles of Scotch, he twisted off the cap and downed it in one fiery gulp. The liquor burned down to his belly, but did little to quench the fire roiling in his blood. He laughed at the tiny bottle, a short, bitter burst of sound that echoed in the barren hotel room. It would take a whole lot more alcohol to drown the memories of this night.

He set the bottle down on the desk and dropped to sit on the bed with a sigh of defeat. Propping his elbows on his knees, he put his head in his hands. His eyes traced a pattern in the nap of the carpet, but it led to no solutions. Rubbing his hands over his face, he pressed fingertips into his eye sockets until spots of color danced behind his lids, sparkling red exactly like Anna's bright hair. He released the pressure in an instant.

He could only blame himself for these complications. He had been too cocky: in the cab, he had had the brilliant idea that if he took her home, he might have one last shot at convincing her. When she turned to him in the dim light of her apartment, he had known it was a mistake. Her kiss had startled him, thrown him off balance, so much so that kissing her back had been inevitable. If only she hadn't tasted so sweet, if her eyes hadn't been filled with such desire. He had tried to retreat, but then she had looked so unhappy and he couldn't resist kissing her again—

He rose to his feet in an impatient surge. It was done. Over. As much as he might want to, he couldn't undo it. Part of him knew he *wouldn't* undo it, that this was the most pleasurable night of love he had ever experienced. He looked at the clock: 3:06 a.m. In four hours, he would be on a jet flying east. He wished he didn't have to wait that long.

Evan stripped off his clothes, noticing the missing button from his shirt and Anna's faint scent lingering on his skin. He stepped into the shower and let the water rinse off the memories as he soaped his body and scrubbed. Tonight, he had violated his creed, the one his father had taught him by deed if not by word: love a woman, yes, but never get attached to one and certainly don't let one get attached to you. Less than an hour from her bed, Evan still felt himself tangled in Anna Berzani's arms.

Shutting off the water, he grabbed a towel. What would the old man do if he were in Evan's situation? Probably pretend tonight never happened. Maybe he should do the same. It wouldn't be hard; the next time he saw Anna would be months from now, maybe even years. He closed his eyes, consoled by the idea, and stretched out in bed. If he was lucky, he could get a couple of hours' sleep.

But sleep eluded him completely. He lay wide-awake in the darkness until the sharp drone of the alarm sounded from the bedside table. He had no luck sleeping on the plane, either, as it lurched and rolled through the summer storms sweeping the country. The plane landed at Baltimore-Washington International without a hitch, but traffic was jammed on the roads outbound. At 5:50 p.m., Evan finally walked into the Laughing Gull, the neighborhood hangout on the banks of Crab Creek, feeling tired, edgy and irritable.

The older man behind the bar looked up from the sports page. "Evan! You look like hell. What's the matter?"

"Hey, George. I had to take a trip out of town. What'd I miss?"

"Not much. Orioles lost another one to Tampa. Get you a beer?"

"Yeah. You still have that summer ale on tap?"

"Sure. Two more kegs. Just for you and the Berzani brothers."

As George was pulling the pint from a tap, Ian Berzani walked into the bar. He greeted his father-in-law and shook Evan's hand. "I got Patty's text about half an hour ago. What's up?"

"We need to revise our strategy. I'll fill you in when Patrick gets here."

"The usual, Ian?" George asked.

"Yeah, thanks, George."

"Might as well pour one for Patrick, too," Evan said. "He should be here any minute."

The older man plucked more glasses from the rack and in a moment slid three beers across the bar. Patrick pushed through the door just as Ian picked up two of the pints.

"You're a mind reader," Patrick said as he took the beer from his brother's hand.

"Like yours is so difficult to read," Evan said with a snort.

"Better than a trip through that cesspool between your ears, McKenzie," Patrick retorted with a grin.

"At least it'd be educational."

"That's not what some would call it."

"Come on, gentlemen," Ian interrupted, enforcing the peace as usual. "Drink first, fight later. Let's grab a table."

George went back to his sports scores. Evan led the way across the room to a table next to the windows. The view from there was spectacular, looking out onto Crab Creek with no obstructions. Better still, just across from the bar, the creek took a bend and opened up to the Chesapeake Bay itself. Though he had seen it hundreds of times, Evan appreciated the sight even more after being away. Ian and Patrick sat down across from him.

"So, what's this powwow about?" Ian asked, sipping his beer.

"Evan crashed and burned, so we need your help," Patrick said. "Which reminds me—pay up, McKenzie." He held out an open palm in Evan's direction.

"What makes you think I choked?" Evan glared at his friend, not wanting to admit the truth.

"If Anna had agreed, I'd know it by now."

"What are you talking about?" Ian narrowed his eyes and shifted his glance between the two of them. "What did you guys do this time?"

Evan ignored the question and dug out his money clip to peel off some bills. "I was *this* close," he said, tossing the money at Patrick. "It was the thought of working with you that spooked her."

"I'll bet it was *you* that had her running scared," Patrick said as he scooped up the money and made a show of counting the five twenties. "Looks like I'm buying, boys."

"Wait a minute," Ian said slowly. "You didn't actually *go* to San Francisco and see Anna did you?"

"What better way to get her aboard?" Patrick asked his brother. He picked up his glass and drank. "McKenzie went. After all, he's the big deal guy."

"That's Master Deal-maker," Evan said, automatically correcting him.

"You two must be time-sharing a brain again," Ian said with a sigh. "What made you think Anna would listen to *him?* She despises Evan."

"She does not," Evan said irritably, remembering just how true that had been, all the while wishing Ian was right.

"Don't kid yourself, McKenzie," Patrick countered. "You two have never had a civil conversation."

"We've had at least one. Over dinner last night," Evan said defensively.

"Doesn't matter. We're back to square one and—" A phone rang, cutting Patrick off. It was his. He dug it out of his shirt pocket. When he checked the screen, his eyebrows rose and he flipped it open. "Hey, Annie. I was just thinking of you. How's my little prodigal sister?"

"Shit." Evan slumped in his seat. Anna wasn't crazy enough to say anything about last night, was she? He listened, but from the side of the conversation Evan could overhear, Patrick seemed to be having the standard brotherly chat with his sister. He took a deep drink of his beer and looked out the windows to the boats on the water in the distance, sails interspersed with the occasional waterman pulling crab traps.

"You're kidding!" Patrick suddenly exclaimed.

He looked right at Evan, his expression one of astonished glee.

Evan cringed in anticipation and slumped farther in his chair.

"I mean, wow! Great! When will you—okay I'll tell them. And hey, Annie? Thanks." Patrick closed his phone and grinned at Evan. "She's going to do it."

"What? No! But she said—" Evan stopped himself abruptly. He straightened in his chair, one hand wrapped tightly around his glass. His stomach was clenched and his throat dry. He wasn't sure which felt stronger: panic or exhilaration. Why had she changed her mind?

"What do you mean 'what?'" Patrick prompted. "Now you sound like you don't want her to do it."

"Forget it. It doesn't matter. Is she coming here?"

"Two weeks, maybe three, she has to arrange her schedule."

Evan swirled the beer in his glass around and around, mimicking the whirling in his brain. He would see Anna sooner than expected. What was he supposed to do? How could he pretend last night never happened? Especially when it was all he could think about. He would have to, though. What other choice did he have?

Patrick shook his head in disbelief. "I guess you *are* the master deal-maker after all."

"Damn straight." Evan pushed the unease to the back of his mind. He would deal with Anna when the time came; there was no point in worrying about it now. Besides, she might want to forget it as much as he did. And he would forget it. He just needed a little time and a good night's sleep. He stuck out his hand and motioned for Patrick to hand over the money. His friend scowled and dug the bills out of his pocket.

The grimace on Patrick's face as he returned the twenties,

then added another hundred dollars from his own wallet, was priceless. Ian grinned as he watched, then laughed.

"There goes the new race-watch I was going to buy myself," Patrick said with a grumble.

Evan wanted to laugh, too, but he couldn't. Despite having won the bet, he had nothing to be happy about. The final reckoning was coming, and no amount of money would cover the bill.

Chapter Four

Anna kept her eyes closed as she sipped a tepid ginger ale. The fizzy liquid hit the bottom of her stomach and sloshed around uncomfortably. After a few moments, it decided to stay put. She sighed in relief, but didn't take another drink. She didn't trust her stomach right now.

She hated the fact that she got motion sick. It was an irritating, embarrassing malady. The illness didn't even occur every time she was in a car, boat or airplane, which made it all the more annoying. It randomly hit when she was least expecting it and often when she could do the least about it. Luckily, the airplane was well stocked with ginger ale for her and other sufferers. Leaning her head back, she willed the nausea roiling in the pit of her stomach to subside.

As she sat in silent misery, it occurred to her that this wasn't ordinary motion sickness. The queasiness had started long before the plane left the ground—several days ago, in fact. This morning, she had thrown up before she had even gotten on the plane. There was a simple answer, but Anna refused to consider it. There was no way it could be true. Despite her stubbornness, the reasoning crept back to plague her all during the long flight. This wasn't motion sickness at all, her subconscious whispered. This was *Evan*-sickness. He was the reason she felt this way. Or, rather, the prospect of seeing him was.

Anna's eyes popped open and she stared at the seat-back in front of her for a minute, before closing them again. It couldn't be true; she wouldn't let it be. But she couldn't deny that the thought of meeting Evan again had her guts strung tighter than a drum. *Three weeks,* she thought as she let her head fall back against the rest. Three weeks and... nothing.

The morning after her night with Evan, Anna awoke, surprised to find herself alone. She had looked at the clock—5:17—then pulled on a robe and gone to the living room. Evan's clothes were gone. Her dress and coat were neatly draped over the back of a chair. The roses he had brought were a bright spark in the dim quiet, but they were the only sign Evan had been there at all. Staring at them, Anna had wrapped her arms around herself, warding off a sudden chill.

She had sat on the sofa, alone, curling her legs under herself. If it hadn't been for the draped clothes and flowers, she could almost believe the previous night had never happened. But it had. The soft ache in her body, the languor in her limbs, told the story more clearly than words or memories. So where had Evan gone? And why had he left without waking her? The possible answers to those questions spread an anxious tension through her body. She had thrust her doubts away. No one could fake the desire he had shown over and over again.

Now, three weeks later, sitting on a jet winging its way east, Anna wasn't so certain. With so many modern ways to communicate, Evan had chosen none: no phone call, no e-mail, no text, no fax, no Tweet. Not even a second-hand message via one of her brothers or—God forbid— her mother. It really was as if the night hadn't happened. Reaching in the pocket of her skirt, Anna pulled out a small white button. It was from a man's shirt and, since the roses had long since faded and died, the only proof she had that Evan had been in her apartment—in her *bed*.

When she had hurried out the door to work that dismal day, the button had skittered away from the toe of her shoe. Retrieving it, she had clenched the disk in her hand until it left a deep imprint in her palm. Anna had carried it with her since, a talisman, a reminder of a dream come true that had vanished like smoke.

Anna sighed and sipped more of the ginger ale. The liquid settled better. She risked eating a pretzel, the salt sharp on her tongue. In a few short hours, she would see Evan and her questions would be answered. Until then, she had to think positive thoughts. She drank the last of her soda and took a deep breath.

The flight attendant announced their final descent into BWI Airport. A few bumpy minutes later, the jet was taxiing to the gate. When the seat-belt sign turned off, Anna collected her belongings, grabbed her suitcase from the overhead bin and joined the hordes bustling through the terminal. She dodged a man and a woman who had stopped to look at the overhead display of arrivals and departures. A few steps on, she wove around a man in a Stetson ambling along with a cell phone pressed to his ear.

Anna paid no attention to the milling crowd of people waiting just beyond the security checkpoint. With no bags to collect, she navigated directly to the car rental counter. Hopefully there wouldn't be a bottleneck there. Her meeting in Crab Creek was scheduled for one o'clock. She was just about to step on the escalator, when a hand grabbed her arm.

"Caught you, Anna Maria!" Astonished, Anna turned her head to see her mother beaming at her. Elaine threw her arms around Anna, hugging her fiercely. "Oh, it is *so* good to see you!"

Anna automatically returned the embrace, then realized that they were blocking everyone's access to the escalator. Elaine didn't seem to care as she drew back and ran her eyes over her youngest. She wouldn't relax until she was sure that her "baby" had all her limbs and no visible scars. Anna rolled her eyes and smiled.

"Ma. Let's get out of—"

"Step aside, lady," a large man said in a gruff voice. "I ain't got all day."

"I'm trying," Anna snapped back. "She's my mother, okay?"

"Nice for you," he said, deadpan. "You're still in the way."

"Mind your manners, young man," Elaine said with a frown. "I haven't seen her in months."

The man blinked, then shifted his bulk. Suddenly, he looked sheepish when faced with the ire of an older woman half his size. "Yes, ma'am," he said politely.

As Anna bit her lip and pulled Elaine away from the escalator a tall, older man with silver-gray hair scooped her into a bear hug that nearly crushed her ribs. His deep, boisterous laugh rang in the airport's main hall.

When she was set back on her feet, Anna gasped for breath. "Pop! What are you doing here? I told you I was renting a car."

Antonio frowned as he regarded his daughter. "Bah, they charge too much here. It is better that we pick you up."

"Of *course* we had to pick you up," Elaine said, nearly over the top of her husband's words. "We couldn't let you arrive without a proper welcome."

"Besides, we have a car you can use," Antonio said. "Whenever you want."

"Except for tomorrow, Tonio. I have my garden-club meeting."

"But otherwise, we don't need it."

"And your father has a doctor's appointment on Thursday," Elaine said with a smile, then echoed her husband, "but otherwise, it's yours."

Anna looked between her parents, laughed a little and gave up. She wouldn't win the argument and it was pointless to try. "I suppose. If there's a conflict, I can always rent one in town."

"Perfetto!" Antonio beamed at her. "Of course there will be no problem. If not our car, there is Patricio's pickup."

"Or Ian's, dear," Elaine reminded him, slipping her arm through Anna's and hugging her close. "I am so *happy* to see you."

"It is good to have you home at last," Antonio said in agreement. "I will get your luggage."

"No need. I just have this," Anna said, shaking her head. Her father took the handle of her bag, looking disappointed that it was so light. She felt compelled to add, "I'm only here for four days."

Elaine frowned. "That's so short. Can't you stay longer?"

"Do not worry, *tesoro,*" Antonio said, patting his wife on the shoulder. "Soon it will be *forever.*"

"Who said *that?*" Anna asked in alarm.

Antonio ignored her. "Come, we are parked over there."

"Pop, I'm only here to help design this project of yours," Anna said firmly as they traversed the sky bridge to the parking tower.

"Not *my* project," Antonio said darkly. "Your brothers want change. What is wrong with things as they are?"

"Because neither Ian nor Patrick wants to run the yard," Anna offered.

"I can still run it," he said indignantly, glaring at her as if the whole thing were her idea. "I built that boatyard from scratch and I know every inch of it. I—"

"Calm down, dear," Elaine said, trotting to keep up with his longer legs.

"I'm only repeating what Evan told me," Anna protested.

"Evan and Patricio. Those two are thick as thieves, as usual." Antonio scowled as he pulled his keys out of his pocket and unlocked a large silver sedan. "They have no respect for me."

"It sounds like they want what's best for you," Anna said as she got in the backseat.

"No. They want what is best for *them*," Antonio said in a growl. "I have no say in this."

"Now, Tonio," Elaine said. "You know that's not true."

Antonio grumbled something in Italian under his breath, started the car and backed it out of the slot. In minutes they were out of the garage and into the sunshine. Elaine kept up a steady stream of chatter about the neighborhood and the town while Antonio continued to sulk and mutter. She threw a question at Anna every once in a while, fishing for information. Anna answered some and deflected others, knowing they would come back around eventually. Her mother was dogged in her inquisitiveness.

When they exited the freeway onto Maple Street, Anna rolled down her window and let the warm air wash over her face. It was more humid than what she was used to in California, but the breeze carried the scents of her childhood: milkweed, joe-pye weed, goldenrod. The sweltering heat of summer was over. Now came the long, lovely autumn that lingered in perfection over the shores of the Chesapeake. It was the season she missed the most; San Francisco had much to commend it, but its fall couldn't match the glory of Maryland's.

As she looked out the window, Anna noticed the new construction, especially near the shores of the Bay. Evan had been right. McMansions lined the water, crowding out the smaller traditional homes. These new owners would welcome a nice restaurant and a few shops in their neighborhood.

Her father turned the car onto Bayshore, which paralleled the water. Soon they came to A&E Marine, tucked behind a tall chain-link fence. As Antonio parked, Anna could see that the boatyard was busy, as usual. In her entire life, she had never seen it idle. Even the winters hummed with activity, though most work was carried on inside, hidden from the casual eye. The action today was outside.

September marked the second rush of the year. From now through early December, boats were hauled, blocked and covered for the winter. Off to the left of the lot, several were already in place on the yellow stands. Of course, some of those had been there for years. The owners never seemed to finish whatever projects they started. Or the list of repairs kept getting longer rather than shorter. Anna was sure they would still be there next spring and the one after that.

Unless there wasn't a boatyard here at all.

The possibility caused a pang in her heart, but just as quickly, she squelched it. Evan was right again: no one wanted to run the yard. Patrick was wrapped up in his wife and daughter and the sailboat racing he enjoyed so much. In a couple of months, Ian was sailing away with his new family on a world circumnavigation. Jeannie had a busy life with her family and the printing business they owned. And Anna had a life far away from Crab Creek.

Getting out of the car, she pulled her briefcase with her. A breeze blew across her face, bringing the smells of the boatyard: the sickly sweet polyester, the acrid varnish and paint. A boat being pressure-washed at the travel lift added the dead-fish scent she knew so well. Despite the strong odors, Anna had to smile. This was forever home, no matter how far away she tried to run.

Her mother got out of the car, and together they walked across the gravel lot to the office, her father following. She got as far as the concrete walkway.

"Hey, Anna-Banana."

Spinning around, she frowned at her brother Patrick. "Didn't you promise never to call me that again?"

"I doubt it," he said with a grin. Patrick dropped the coil of exhaust hose he carried and gave her a hug. "Doesn't sound like me at all."

Anna laughed and returned her brother's embrace. "You're right. It was probably Ian. He's the only nice one in this family."

"Nice is overrated. Hey, Pop. Hey, Ma. How's the traffic?"

"Terrible, as usual," Antonio said. "The construction on the interchange is horrible. Is that for Buckman's boat?" Antonio pointed to the hose.

Patrick frowned and picked up the coil, carrying it over and leaning it against the side of the building. "It was. But it's the wrong size."

As Patrick and his father began arguing about what to do with the hose, another deep voice hailed Anna from across the parking lot. She took a few steps, meeting Ian in a hug. "Hey, big brother."

"Good to see you, Annie. How was the jet stream?"

"Bumpy. How's Mimi?" Ian had married one of Anna's best friends the year before.

"Good." Stepping back, Ian gave her a once-over. "Looking pretty professional there, sis."

Anna tugged at her suit jacket a bit self-consciously. She had dressed her part carefully, in a summer-weight wool suit in light brown with a subtle cream plaid running through the fabric. With an ivory blouse, brown leather heels and matching accessories, she looked the businesswoman she hoped her family would mistake her for.

"I thought the suit would help cut down on the family arguments," she said, lowering her voice. "And keep the discussions on the business at hand."

"With Ma and Pop there?" Ian grinned, his dark brown eyes sparkling with humor. "Good luck on that."

She punched him in the arm. "Thanks for the vote of confidence."

"Better to start out expecting the worst," Ian said with a shrug. He put an arm over her shoulder and led her toward the others. "By the way, Mimi and I want you to come to dinner tomorrow night."

"No," Antonio said abruptly. "Tomorrow *I* cook. You will all eat."

"Is that an invitation or an order?" Ian asked, raising one dark eyebrow.

"The charm just oozes out of him, doesn't it?" Anna said and her brothers laughed.

"You, Anna Maria," her father said, wagging a finger at her, "are a very disrespectful child."

"That's not a news flash, Pop," Patrick said.

"And *child* isn't exactly right," Ian said. He looked down at Anna and added, "Though you've been child*ish* more than once."

A short jab into her brother's ribs had him dropping his arm off her shoulders and wincing away with a laugh. "Come to dinner with us the night after, then."

"And Kate's expecting you tonight," Patrick said.

"I can feel my waistline expanding already." Anna smiled up at her two brothers, happy to see them. They had turned out to be good men—an outcome greatly in doubt during her childhood.

"Let's get the fireworks started," Ian said. "I've got varnish to get back to."

He turned toward the office as Anna asked, "Where's Jeannie?"

"She's running late. As usual." Patrick's lips twitched. "But she called to say she's on her way and we should start without her."

"How generous of her," Anna said drily. She knew her older sister would love to miss the conflagration altogether.

"Where's McKenzie?" Ian asked Patrick. "He's never late."

Patrick frowned. "I don't know. I—"

His words were interrupted by the squeal of tires on pavement. A red convertible zipped around the corner and shot through the gates into the yard. Gravel spattered from under its tires as it roared to a halt in front of the office. Low and sleek, there was nothing subtle about the car. Sparkling paint, shining chrome, black leather interior: the car looked like sin on four wheels. The driver revved the engine once, then twice before putting it in Park and turning off the key.

"Look out. Mario McKenzie's testing product again," Patrick observed, his arms crossed over his chest.

"It just came in this morning," Evan said with a grin. His eyes were shaded by wraparound dark glasses, making him look as dangerous as the car. He got out, tossing the sunglasses on the dashboard. "If you're nice, I'll let you take it for a spin later."

As soon as Anna saw Evan, every muscle in her body tensed. He was as gorgeous as she remembered, especially now that she had firsthand knowledge of all the hot, hard skin hiding under the tailored gray suit and crisp white shirt. Her stomach churned again, threatening to embarrass her. Swallowing down bile, Anna tried to relax.

She waited for him to turn his attention her way, heart pounding. He seemed to ignore her, though. He greeted Patrick and Ian first, then came around the car to shake Antonio's hand and kiss Elaine's cheek. He had a joke, a smile and word for everyone. When he finally turned to her, her breath caught. His green eyes were guarded, his face expressionless.

"Anna." He nodded once, a short, sharp gesture. "Uh… how's it going? I didn't think I'd see you so soon."

"Really?" Anna raised an eyebrow. "I told Patrick three weeks ago I'd be here."

"Yeah. Right. I guess he mentioned that," Evan said, fiddling with his keys. He paused, then added, "Before, I meant."

"Before what?"

Evan cleared his throat. "You said you weren't going to design the project, when we were in—" He stopped, looking uncomfortable.

Anna waited, but he didn't continue. She couldn't believe this. He couldn't even say the *words?* "In San Francisco? When I saw you last time? Over *dinner?*"

"Uh, yeah. There."

"Well, she's here now," Patrick interrupted. "And *you* finally showed up, McKenzie."

"Unlike some people, I have a life," Evan gibed Patrick with a grin, animation once more filling his face.

"Is that what you call it?" Patrick shot back. "Come on, let's get started."

Evan followed Patrick toward the office door as they tossed quips back and forth in their usual style. Watching him walk away, hurt disbelief locked Anna in place. She couldn't—didn't *want* to—believe what had just occurred. But it was too clear and unavoidable. It explained the three weeks of silence: Evan obviously regretted their night together. His stilted words and uncomfortable fidgeting spoke volumes.

Now what was she going to do? There was nothing between them, not even the bond of one night's passion. Her father tugged Anna's arm. Still stunned, furious, on the verge of tears, she let him guide her into the office and under the sign above the door that read A&E Marine.

EVAN STRUGGLED TO KEEP the casual, customary stream of conversation flowing between him and Patrick. Inside the office, out of the revealing sunlight, he moved around the counter that stretched across the front. Retreating to the back of the room, he stood next to the filing cabinets that covered one wall. Patrick pushed some paperwork aside on one of the two desks that faced each other in the center of the space. He propped himself there, one leg swinging. Elaine came in and swatted his leg, as if to correct his bad manners, but he only grinned and stayed where he was.

Evan leaned against one of the cabinets and stared out the window at the boatyard. He wished he could get in his car and speed away. He had been crazy to think he could pull this off. One look at Anna and his pulse went into overdrive; his palms itched with the need to touch her. All the memories of their night together had come flooding back, no matter how deep he had buried them—or *thought* he had.

He rubbed a hand over his face. God, he had sounded like such an *idiot*. Anna thought so, too, he could tell.

Pretending there was nothing between them was going to be harder than he had thought. Maybe impossible. Turning back to the room, Evan vowed to keep better control of himself.

Anna and her father had squared off against each other in the center of the room. They were arguing about something already, each wearing identical expressions of stubborn intent. Jeannie burst through the door and there was the usual commotion of greetings. The oldest Berzani child, Jeannie shared Elaine's red hair and short stature. Finally, Anna seized control of the chaos and got the meeting started. Jeannie stood with her elbows on the counter and rested her chin on her hand, obviously expecting the entertainment to begin. She was not disappointed.

"You mean you didn't look at the questions I sent you?" Anna asked.

"Why would I? That is what we are here for today," Antonio said, his annoyance matching Anna's. "We decide for all of us."

Anna put her hands on her hips. "This is a total waste of my time. I can't believe I said I'd get involved."

"Now you don't have time for your family?" he asked, frowning at her.

"Right now, you're not my family. You're a *client*."

"You might live ten thousand miles away, Anna Maria," Elaine said, narrowing her eyes at her youngest child, "but we will *always* be a family."

"Ma, that's not what I meant!"

Evan could practically see steam whistling from Anna's ears. He tried to ignore the fact that she looked gorgeous, holding her ground in the center of another Berzani family "discussion." A becoming flush had risen to her cheeks and her eyes sparkled dangerously. Seconds later, Patrick opened his mouth and sided with his parents against Anna, escalating the melee. Jeannie threw in comments, as well, irritating her father and Anna impartially. As usual, Ian waited patiently for the opportunity to restore peace. Evan found himself irritated with all of them for giving Anna such a hard time.

"We're all family here," he said, coming to Anna's defense. "No one's disputing that. Let's focus on the project."

"There's a concept." Anna turned, her eyes narrowing as she glared at him coldly. "So, what's the deal here, Evan? *You* were the one who said we had deadlines to meet. I assumed you'd at least keep everything moving forward."

"Hold on, Annie," Ian said, finally jumping in. "Evan's been swamped with work. *We've* barely seen him since he got back."

"Well, it's reassuring to know I'm not the only one being ignored," she said.

Her eyes held Evan's captive. He saw a flash of pain before it was quickly shuttered. That glimpse jolted him. All the justifications for not calling her came flooding back. In that instant, he knew they were lies, put up only to buttress his own sanity. His head started to ache, a dull throb of tension.

"Get real, Annie," Patrick said with a grin. "Did you actually think you could blow in, get your job done in a day and then get out?"

"I *expected* you to have something for me to work with. Something more substantial than a family feud."

"It's not feuding, Annie. It's called *bonding*," Jeannie said drily.

"It's aggravating is what it is. Why did I ever say I would do this?"

"Because you couldn't resist McKenzie's charm?" Patrick asked, cocking his head to one side.

"That must be my only excuse," she said softly and turned her merciless eyes back on Evan. "He lured me in with false promises and here I am."

She was baiting him—Evan knew it—but the urge to explain, to defend himself, swept over him anyway. He wrestled the compulsion into submission. He had gone to bed with Anna from love or lust or whatever selfish reason of the moment. Pretending it didn't happen was the smartest avenue to take. She wouldn't see it the same way, but he was trying to do what was best for both of them. He could never be tied to any woman and Anna would never be happy with a short-term fling. It was over. It had to be.

"This is a family business, Anna," Antonio said, drawing everyone's attention from Evan. "Your mother and I built it for our children. Now we must change it so that our children will take it over from us."

"Pop, please. You don't—"

"No." Antonio held up a hand to stop Anna's protest. "I accept this. But I also have little interest in what will be. I am too old for that. I only want a place that will bring all my children together." His gaze encompassed them all, even Evan.

"We know that you all want what is best for us," Elaine said quietly. She moved to stand next to Antonio who put an arm across her shoulders. "And we want what is best for you, too. That's why we've agreed to this. It doesn't mean that it's easy."

Silence held for a long moment, rare for such a boisterous, voluble family. Evan watched as the siblings traded glances. Finally, Ian broke through the stasis.

"Well, Annie, go ahead. What's your first question?"

Anna sighed, picked up her briefcase and popped the

latches. Taking out a yellow tablet and a pen, she turned and sat at the desk where Patrick perched.

"All right. Who wants condos? Raise your hand."

Chapter Five

Rolling onto her back, Anna sighed and fought consciousness. It was no use; her body thought it was still in San Francisco and would not let her sleep. Her eyes slid open and she yawned, stretching her arms across the expanse of the bed. For an instant, she remembered waking alone the morning after her passionate night with Evan. She had been so confused then. She was no less so *this* morning.

Yesterday, after he had greeted her so stiffly, she had wished she could be anywhere but in that office, stuck with him and her family. Even when the meeting began to go well, she had been wary. Then argument changed to a true discussion between everyone. Strangely, she and Evan seemed to be on the same wavelength. As the debate continued, the others dropped out. Finally, it had been just her and Evan talking. For a few minutes, Anna had felt exhilarated, in tune with his feelings and thoughts. In a way, it was as intimate as sex.

That brief closeness had bewildered her. It had occurred to her that maybe he *didn't* regret what happened after all. Maybe he was just confused and hiding his feelings in front of her family. But then, as soon as the meeting was over, he disappeared. One minute he was there, the next gone without a word, leaving her with no clue as to his feelings for her and no idea what she should think or do about him.

Pushing the covers to one side, Anna sat up and put her feet on the floor. A wave of nausea washed over her. "Whoa," she said aloud, putting a hand to her mouth and swallowing hard. Like the day before, the bile would not be held back. She made a dash for the bathroom and crouched over the porcelain while her stomach upended itself.

When the queasiness had settled, she rinsed her mouth and brushed her teeth. After washing her face, she patted it dry with a towel, looking at her pale self in the mirror. "No more thinking about Evan before breakfast," she told her reflection.

She put down the towel and pulled on her old, comfy but tattered bathrobe that her mother had preserved and hung on the back of the door, then went out to face her parents. In the hall outside her bedroom, the aroma of her father's Italian-roast coffee hit her. Usually a tantalizing treat, this morning it smelled suspicious and she wrinkled her nose.

Swallowing down nausea, Anna continued down the stairs and past the living and dining rooms. From the back of the house, she heard the low rumble of her father's voice, followed by the lighter ring of her mother's. Pushing open the swinging kitchen door, she stepped into a room bright with sunshine and full of the scents of cooking.

Her father had his back to her as he presided at the stove, stirring a pan of what had to be peppers, onions and new potatoes. He would add eggs on the side, along with toast for a filling breakfast to celebrate her return. He was humming an aria from an obscure Giordano opera.

"Good morning," Elaine said brightly. "How did you sleep?"

"'Morning, Ma," Anna said, pressing a kiss to her

mother's cheek, then doing the same for her father. "'Morning, Pop. I slept great."

"There is coffee. I ground the beans fresh," Antonio said, cracking eggs into a second pan on the stove and reaching over to depress the toaster button. "Breakfast is coming soon."

"Just toast for me," Anna said, sliding into a chair at the table.

"What?" Elaine frowned. "Don't you feel well?"

Anna rolled her eyes. "Just because I only want toast doesn't mean I'm sick."

"But it's your father's special breakfast," her mother said, coming around the table to lay a hand on Anna's forehead and cheeks, checking for fever. In Elaine's book, serious illness was the only explanation for not eating. "You do look pale this morning. Did you eat something at Patrick and Kate's that didn't agree with you?"

"I'm *fine*, Ma." Anna smiled up at her mother, trying to project reassurance. "I was just a little queasy this morning, that's all. Probably too much red wine last night."

"Hmm." Her mother was obviously unconvinced. "You should eat. It will make you feel better."

At that moment, Antonio slid a plate in front of her. It was all Anna could do to keep her composure. The fried eggs, gleaming with oil, made her stomach do a slow roll. She swallowed and smiled at her father as he set out another plate for Elaine, then sat with his own breakfast.

"Your mother is right," he said. "Eggs soak up the excess wine and convert it to vitamins. Don't laugh! It is true."

Averting her eyes as he cut into his eggs, Anna picked up a piece of dry toast. Taking a small bite, she chewed and swallowed. Her system accepted the morsel, so she took another bite. Elaine rose and poured coffee into a cup for Anna before refilling Antonio's and her own mug.

The smell of the dark brew was even worse up close. Anna could practically feel herself turn green. Pushing the cup discreetly to the side, she nibbled on the harmless toast.

"Delicious, as usual, my dear," Elaine said with a smile at Antonio. She eyed Anna who hastily speared a slice of potato and smiled back. Elaine pursed her lips. "I hope you weren't driving under the influence last night, Anna Maria."

"She's Italian," Antonio said sternly. "She can hold her wine. It's genetic."

"Don't forget, she's Irish, too," Elaine countered.

"As long as she stays away from the whiskey, then." Antonio winked at Anna.

"Try a little egg, Anna," her mother urged. "Protein is good for hangovers."

"Ma, I am not hungover," Anna protested, rolling her eyes.

"Then what's the matter?" Elaine mused aloud. "Let's hope you're not pregnant." She turned to her husband. "Do you remember, Tonio, when I could tell I was pregnant just by smelling coffee in the morning? One whiff and I was in the bathroom."

Antonio chuckled. "Better than any test on a rabbit, that is certain."

Elaine laughed and sipped her coffee, then started gossiping about the latest boatyard drama: two of the employees were having a feud and could no longer work together. The story required no response, which was good, because Anna's brain had clamped down on one word.

Pregnant.

Pregnant?

Pregnant!

The word raced around in her head like a gerbil on a wheel, circling and circling, faster and faster, but going nowhere. It couldn't be true, it just couldn't. As she did the calculations in her head, Anna's stomach clenched again. Sweat broke out across her forehead and dampened her palms. It *was* possible—more than possible. In fact, the math was just about perfect. But how? She was on the *pill*. Its failure rate was infinitesimally small, wasn't it?

"You don't look so good." Antonio's deep voice seemed to come from a long distance away.

"Anna? Sweetheart?" Elaine got up and came around the table to crouch at her daughter's side. "What's wrong?" She smoothed Anna's hair back from her face and their eyes met.

Anna could only stare at her mother, mute. She tried to smile, but tears clogged her throat. She had no words to explain, nor did she dare try. It was as if by not speaking, she could keep the truth from crashing down around her.

Elaine's face was taut with worry as she searched her daughter's face. Then her gray gaze sharpened with alarmed comprehension. Anna could almost hear the gears turning and knew that her mother had answered her own question.

"Are you certain?" Elaine asked softly.

"What is wrong with her?" Antonio asked in a gruff tone. He rose to his feet and towered over the two women. "We should take her to the hospital."

Anna shook her head slowly from side to side. She could speak again, but the words wouldn't come out in any sensible order. "I don't... I just... I can't—"

Taking Anna's hands in hers, Elaine squeezed them gently. Her grip was warm and firm against the cold numbness that affected Anna right now. "We can find out today," Elaine said with a gentle smile. "This morning. I'll call for an appointment right now."

"Will someone tell me what is wrong?" Antonio's voice

rose to a bellow. He put a hand on Anna's shoulder, turning her to face him. Tears rose and spilled over her lower lashes as Anna looked up at her father. With a growl of empathy, he gathered her in his arms and held her tightly. "Just tell me, Anna Maria, and I will make it better."

The comforting, familiar words only made the tears flow faster. When she was small, her father had always stood between her and the world. He had an answer to any question, a solution for any problem and was always ready to protect her. This time, though, there was nothing he could do.

Antonio patted her back as she wept. "She is crying," he said to Elaine over Anna's head. His tone was accusatory.

"Don't worry, dear," Elaine said.

"But something must be causing her to suffer!"

"Not necessarily. I cried all the time when I was pregnant. Remember?"

Anna felt Antonio stiffen as his wife's words registered. She pulled away from her father's embrace. Wiping her cheeks with the sleeve of her robe, she struggled for composure. Elaine made a clucking sound and handed her a napkin. After Anna had blown her nose, she reluctantly met her father's eyes. It was the hardest thing she had ever done; his disappointment was going to hurt both of them.

Antonio's dark eyes were narrowed; his expression unreadable. Putting his hands on her shoulders, he surveyed her face carefully. "Who is he?"

The question confused Anna. "What?"

"Who did this to you?" Antonio's question was nearly a growl. "Tell me."

If he hadn't looked so angry and determined, Anna would have laughed. The question was completely ridiculous. "No one *got* me pregnant, Pop."

Antonio frowned and gave her a little shake. "You are not alone in this, Anna Maria. I will not have my daughter—"

"I'm an adult, Pop," she interrupted. "I take full responsibility for my actions and their consequences."

"As will he," her father said ominously, dropping his grip. "I will see to it."

Anna rolled her eyes. "First of all, we don't even know if it's true and if it is—"

"I know it's true," Elaine said calmly, and began to stack the plates.

Anna fidgeted with the tie on her robe. Her mother's calm acceptance was a balm. "I can't be pregnant, Ma."

"Is that so?" Elaine asked as she took the dishes to the sink. "Well, go get dressed anyway, dear. I'll call Dr. Maguire's office and get you in to see her this morning."

Antonio glowered first at Anna, then at his wife. "No one has told me who has fathered this child."

"We'll figure that out later." Elaine patted his arm before she picked up the phone. "It's not as if the baby's going anywhere."

"Elaine! This is not a game. The honor of our daughter and our family is at stake," Antonio roared at his wife.

"Quiet, dear. I'm on the phone," Elaine scolded.

Anna used the moment to retreat from the kitchen and go upstairs to her bedroom. There, she sank onto the bed and dropped her head into her hands. The nausea had abated, but she still felt cold and clammy. Severe shock did that to a person, she had read once. How could she be *pregnant?*

The temptation to crawl back between the soft sheets and pull the covers over her head was strong. But hiding wasn't going to help. Rising, she went into the bathroom, dropped her robe and turned on the shower. Standing under the warm water, Anna ran a hand over her perfectly flat stomach.

Anna knew in her heart what the doctor would say. What she would do with the truth, she didn't know. One thing was certain: her night with Evan could never be wished—or pretended—away. No matter what he or she wanted, they were bound together. It was as certain as the life that had begun to grow inside her.

ELAINE STOPPED THE SEDAN in front of the house and turned off the engine. As she and Anna got out of the car, her mother kept up a steady stream of inconsequential chatter that was simultaneously soothing and irritating. Soothing, because Elaine had not asked about the results of the pregnancy test. Annoying, because the question was sure to come; the chatter was just a delaying tactic. It would be better if Elaine just asked and got it over with quickly, like pulling off a Band-Aid in one quick rip of skin and hair follicles.

"I hope your father remembered to turn on the oven. Those beans need at least three hours to simmer."

At the mention of Antonio, Anna stopped ten feet from the house. She knew he was lurking inside, ready to pounce on her the instant she set foot through the door. Her mother might have a tactful side, but her father certainly didn't. She just couldn't face him right now.

"I'm going to drive over and see if Mimi's around, okay?" Before Elaine could object, Anna had plucked the keys out of her hand.

Elaine smiled as if she understood her daughter's motivation. "That's fine, dear. You know where I'll be."

"I'll be back in a while to give you a hand setting up for tonight."

"Take your time. I'm sure you two have some catching up to do."

In minutes, Anna was pushing open the door to the Laughing Gull. Luck was with her: Mimi was just putting a beer down in front of a customer at the bar.

"Anna!" The other woman dashed out from behind the counter and they embraced warmly. "I hoped you'd stop by this afternoon, but I figured your mom would have you wrapped up tight."

"She tried. She likes to wring every possible second of mothering out of my visits," Anna said with a smile. Ruefully, she realized she was giving Elaine a real dose this time. "Can you take a break?"

"You bet. Let me call Dad and have him come over."

"Oh, but—"

"It's not a problem," Mimi interrupted with a laugh. "He said he was going to putter around the house. By this time, Mom's probably ready to get him out of her hair. Go sit down. Can I bring you a drink?"

"Just a lemonade."

Mimi hurried off. Anna found an empty table and sat. It was no accident that she chose the one farthest away from the bar and any other customer in the Gull. The table was next to a large window overlooking Crab Creek. She let her gaze rest on the water, hoping the smooth surface would soothe her turbulent spirits. In what seemed like moments, Mimi was back with two glasses and a dish of pretzels. She slid into the seat opposite Anna.

"Welcome back," Mimi said with a grin. Her blue eyes shone with happiness. "Temporarily, anyway."

"And that's all it's ever going to be."

"And don't you forget it," Mimi finished in unison with Anna.

Both women laughed. When they were girls, they had

spent long hours scheming and dreaming about leaving Crab Creek. Both had escaped, but after ten years, Mimi had returned. Now she was off on a second adventure with Ian that would take her farther away. Anna felt a pang of sadness. With Mimi gone, visits to Crab Creek would not be as fun.

Anna shook off the gloomy thought and asked Mimi how preparations for the voyage were going. More than a week had passed since they spoke over the phone, so in addition to describing all the stuff Ian and she had done on the boat, her son Jack's antics had to be recounted, too. Mimi had a sense of humor for the whole process, which was good since outfitting a small boat for months at sea required a strong one.

They worked their way through the drinks and the pretzels with equal alacrity. When the glasses were empty, George Green appeared at their table.

"Get you ladies another round?"

"Mr. Green!" Anna stood and gave the older man a hug.

"Why, look at you! You haven't changed a bit. Welcome home. How about one of my special margaritas, Annie?" he asked with a twinkle in his eyes. "Since you're finally old enough to drink in here."

Anna grinned, but shook her head. "Just lemonade for me. I have to be on my toes for tonight."

"What? For a barbeque?" Mimi asked. "I thought you required alcohol when the clan gathered."

"Yes, but this is a business trip," Anna said lightly.

"All right." George nodded and picked up the glasses. "Another round coming up."

He left the table and both women watched him leave, then Mimi turned to Anna. "I didn't mean to imply that you drank too much around—"

"And that's not how I took it." Anna laid a hand over her friend's and squeezed.

Mimi turned her hand and gripped Anna's. "What's wrong, Annie? I've been doing all the talking, but I get the impression you have something you want to say."

"Not really. I just—" Anna stopped and looked out the window again, then back at her friend. If she couldn't tell Mimi the truth, who could she tell?

"I'm pregnant."

Mimi's mouth dropped open. "Whoa."

George chose that moment to return with the drinks. He set them on coasters. "Sure I can't tempt you, Annie? My peach margaritas are near perfect."

"Not for me," Anna said softly.

Keeping her eyes on Anna, Mimi nodded. "Bring *me* one. I definitely need a drink."

George looked from one woman to the other, a concerned frown darkening his face. "Is everything okay?"

"Everything's great," Mimi shot him a quick smile.

He paused, then nodded and left the table. Anna looked over at Mimi, her smile a bit lopsided, near to tears as she was. "I'm not supposed to drink when I'm pregnant."

"Don't worry. I'll drink for both of us." Mimi ran a hand through her sandy-brown hair, pulling it loose from her ponytail, and leaned forward over the table. "First, let me ask, are you sure?"

"As sure as a doctor's blood test can be." Anna took a sip of her lemonade, letting the cold liquid slide down her dry throat. "If throwing up this morning and yesterday failed to convince me. God, and three days ago, too."

Anna put her hands over her face. Reality was starting to sink in and panic flooded through her. What was she going to *do?* How could she be pregnant? What had she ever done to deserve this? Sucking in a deep breath, she held it for a moment, then let it out slowly, remembering the answer: she had done one thing, one night, and it had felt so right. And now? Dropping her hands she forced a smile as she looked over at Mimi.

"Except I wasn't. Sure, I mean."

"Huh? I don't understand."

"I didn't connect the dots, so to speak. I just thought I was nervous about seeing—" She stopped and fiddled with the straw in her glass. An image of Evan popped into her mind, not that he was ever far out of it, especially today. She felt a blush suffuse her face and couldn't meet Mimi's gaze.

"About seeing who?"

Anna shook her head and waved away the question with her hand. "Silly me. Working with my parents is stressful, you know?"

Mimi was silent, looking at her through narrowed eyes. "Right."

Anna squirmed under her friend's intent stare. Mimi knew her too well to accept the evasion.

"So how did it happen?" Mimi asked, letting the explanation slide. "I can't believe you weren't using birth control."

"Who knew the twenty-four-hour flu would make such a mess of my life?" Anna's attempt at humor fell flat and she shrugged. "At least that's what the doctor thought the culprit might be."

"Oh, boy." Mimi looked at her, sympathy brimming in her eyes.

George appeared with a tray carrying two stemmed glasses. He set them on the table, ice cubes clinking in the pale peach-colored liquid. A lime wedge decorated the salt encrusted rim. "Two peach margaritas. You looked like you needed one, too, Annie."

Anna touched him on the arm, appreciating his gesture. "Thanks, Mr. Green."

He eyed her for another moment, seeming about to speak, then shook his head. He put a basket of tortilla chips between them along with a small bowl of salsa. "Here's an appetizer to complete the festivities. Can I get you anything else?"

Anna smiled up at him, noting his keen gaze, so much like his daughter's. "This looks great."

From the expression on his face, he didn't buy her cheerfulness, either. But he patted her shoulder and left them alone without another word. Mimi took a sip of her drink, then set the glass back down.

"Who's the lucky father?" she asked bluntly.

"There isn't one."

Mimi giggled, stirring the ice around in her glass. Her dark blue eyes were full of impish humor. "Not another trip to Bethlehem? Should I alert the media?"

"Don't you dare," Anna said with a laugh. "You'll blow my cover." She shook her head and toyed with the straw in her margarita. She wished she could wallow in alcohol and forget this day. Sighing, she pushed the glass to the side. "I just meant I'll be flying solo on this one."

"Does he know?"

"Since I just found out this morning," Anna said drily. "That would be a no."

"So. Are you going to tell him?"

Anna looked away, out the window. Her gaze caught on a sailboat that was slowly creeping into the creek, white canvas bright in the sunshine. "Yes." She turned back to Mimi. "He deserves to know. But I don't expect anything from him."

"Why not?"

Anna shrugged. "I just don't."

"He's not a bastard, you know. At least not one hundred percent. Sure, he's got the attitude, but I think it's a cover. Sometimes, I can't help but like him."

Anna froze, her gaze locked with Mimi's. She could feel the blood drain out of her cheeks as she stared. "Who are you talking about?"

Mimi was silent, then put her hands out and grasped Anna's. "The father of your baby," she said gently, her eyes filled with kindness. "Evan McKenzie."

Reflexively, at the sound of the name, Anna's hands tightened on Mimi's. They were an anchor she badly needed right now. Tears filled her eyes and she squeezed them shut tightly. She didn't know how her friend had figured out the truth, but she was glad that Mimi knew.

"What am I going to do?" Anna whispered.

"Take a deep breath, stop panicking and tell me what I can do to help."

Anna followed orders, though the panic only receded a little. "Let's see. Can you turn back the clock three weeks?" she asked, trying to joke about it.

"Sorry. That I *can't* do." Mimi shook her head ruefully. "I can be with you when you tell him, if you want."

Anna sighed. "No, I'd rather not have an audience for that horror show."

"You never know. He might be excited when he hears."

With a snort, Anna shook her head. "Not likely. No, he's going to freak out that our one-night stand had permanent consequences. I can't say I blame him," she finished softly. "I'm a little freaked, too. *More* than a little, truthfully."

"It'll get easier." Mimi patted Anna's hand and took a sip of margarita. "Just wait. Soon wonder will set in. Then anticipation. I think that's why it takes so long to have a baby—to give you time to adjust to the big change. And trust me, nine months is an incredibly long time."

"What did Johnny do when you told him?" Anna asked, though she knew the man who had fathered Mimi's child had left them both after Jack was born.

"Oh, he was excited." Mimi shook her head, her expression wry. "It was *afterward* that he got scared. He was the best expectant father imaginable. He rubbed my feet, brought me weird food at three in the morning. Anything I wanted, he bent over backward to do. But when he held Jack for the first time, the look on his face was one of utter and complete terror."

"I don't think Evan's going to be a great expectant father."

"Maybe it's better if he isn't." Mimi twirled her glass on the table. "He'll be the opposite of Johnny."

"If only men were that simple to predict."

Both women laughed. Anna dipped a fingertip into her margarita, then dabbed at the salt on the rim of her glass. Transferring the grains to her tongue, she let them melt there, savoring the sharp bite. She looked over at Mimi again.

"How did you figure it out?"

"About Evan?" Mimi shook her head with a laugh. "Ian mentioned that he'd gone out to see you a few weeks ago. Knowing that you haven't been dating anyone else lately, he was the first person I thought of. Plus, I saw you giving him the eye at our wedding."

"I was not!"

"Liar," Mimi said. She took a drink, then licked the salt off her lips. Her eyes were sparkling with teasing glee. "I've caught him looking at you, too. Like a cheetah looks at a gazelle."

"I don't… He doesn't…" Anna stammered to a stop,

feeling a hot wash of color rise like a tide in her cheeks. "Really?"

Mimi giggled. "Trust me."

Anna ran a hand through her hair. "This is ridiculous. We sound like we're back in high school."

"No matter how it feels right now, it isn't the end of the world, Annie. Really. It can be a wonderful beginning."

"I hope you're right." Anna sighed, not sure she could believe her friend. "Don't tell anyone, okay? About Evan? Not even Ian."

"Sure."

"I know I'm asking you to keep a secret from your husband—"

"About something that doesn't concern him," Mimi finished. "It's okay, Annie. You and Evan need to figure this out together."

"There's a concept." Anna rubbed her forehead. "Poor Evan. This is really going to be a shock."

"He'll get over it."

Anna wished she could be as certain as her friend. All day, she had been bracing herself for the coming storm. Time after time, she had warned herself of the worst possibilities: his horror, revulsion, panic, anger. At the same time, some irrepressible part of her wished for the opposite, that Evan would feel happy, loving and proud like a father-to-be was supposed to feel. But she had to bury that fantasy deep. False hope did her no good.

She knew exactly what she had to do next: find Evan and tell him. She owed him that much. After that, she would see where they stood. And knowing how gossip and speculation gushed through her family, she had to tell him before someone else did.

Chapter Six

Evan scanned the contract one of his salesmen brought him. His cell phone chimed. Ignoring it, he read through the terms of the deal, then handed it back to the other man.

"Trade-in's got some miles. We'll have trouble selling it off the lot."

"Nah," Brett said. "The jobber will take it off our hands."

"What makes you think that?"

Brett shrugged. "I called him."

"Getting ahead of me, aren't you?"

"Just trying to close the deal, boss."

Evan had to chuckle at the mock-obsequious tone. "Go forth, then, and sell more cars." He waved a hand, shooing Brett away.

The other man grinned, gave a snappy salute and left the office. Evan pulled out his phone to check the text message that had been left. It was from Patrick: *meet @ pops 1245*. Evan frowned. The phone rang and Antonio's number flashed on the screen.

"Hey, Pop," Evan said, answering the call. "I just got a message from Patrick. Says there's a big conference?"

"You must come." Antonio's voice was too large for the phone and boomed out. Evan held it away from his ear a foot and could still hear the older man clearly. "It is urgent."

"What's this about?"

"I will tell you in one half of an hour." Antonio's accent was thick, hinting at how aggravated he was. "The men of this family must act!"

The phone went dead. Shaking his head, Evan couldn't help laughing at Antonio's drama. The phone rang again before he could put it down. This time it was Ian's number on the display. What the hell was going on? Evan sighed and sat back in his chair. Something had stirred up the Berzanis.

Punching the green button, he said, "Hey, Pop just called. What's going on?"

"I'm not sure," Ian answered. "Anna's done something to piss him off."

"Must be the project."

"Maybe. Could be anything, though. You know how well they get along in a confined space."

"His timing stinks," Evan said with an irritated sigh. "We're swamped right now."

The showroom was indeed busy this morning. Leaving would be a problem, but that was the least of Evan's reluctance. He simply did *not* want to get mixed up in another mess that involved Anna Berzani.

"You know Pop. The bigger his audience, the better. But whatever's got him stewed, Patrick and I can probably manage it without you."

"Yeah, tell that to your dad," Evan said with a snort. "I can hear him now—'You have let me down in my hour of need. I expected better of you.'"

"Like you haven't heard it before?" Ian asked with a chuckle. There was a pause, then he added, "I can't blame you for wanting to avoid Anna. She sure laid into you yesterday."

Evan stiffened and leaned forward in his chair. He had a sudden sense that Ian was fishing for something. The suspicion made the hairs on the back of Evan's neck stand straight up. What had Ian noticed to make him throw out this lure?

"She was a bit worked up," he said as casually as he was able.

"I'll say. I was surprised you didn't bite back."

Swiveling around to face the windows, Evan didn't really see the neat rows of shiny new cars laid out on the lot. Absently, he tapped his fingers on the armrest in an effort to channel some of his unease.

"I figured I should minimize the bloodshed." He forced a laugh. "Hell, she and Pop had squared off already. One duel-to-the-death per day is all the family can take."

Ian chuckled. "True enough."

"I'll shake loose of this place for a while and head over to the house," he said more calmly than he felt. "We'll get Pop settled down before he scalps Anna."

"Sounds good," Ian said easily. "See you there."

Disconnecting the call, Evan slipped the phone into his pocket. A vision of Anna Berzani rose in his mind as clearly as if she were standing in his office: the businesswoman in suit and heels. The image quickly dissolved. Or rather, Anna's clothes did. She lay on her bed in San Francisco. Her tousled red curls were spread across white pillows. Her smoldering chocolate eyes beckoned and her skin was flushed with passion. The memory brought arousal rearing its insistent head. Evan groaned.

Closing his eyes, he forced the phantom woman away. When he opened them again, he stared hard at the car lot outside. Red, black, blue, silver: the vehicles represented his kingdom. They were real. Anna was a fantasy. One unbelievable night hadn't changed that fact. Another reality was that Evan had been born a bachelor. He would always be one. He couldn't fool himself into believing anything different.

Evan left his office, determined to hold on to that truth. He would go to the Berzanis' and help put out Antonio's little fire. He had spent too much time lately avoiding the family, feeling as if he had betrayed them, even though they had no idea of his deceit. This was another chance to atone for his misdeed. At least his secret was safe for now; the spotlight would be turned on Anna.

As he walked through the showroom, one of his salesmen was chatting with a customer. John held up his hand as if to wave, but his thumb was tucked against his palm. Evan gave an inward sigh. The discreet signal meant the prospect was on the fence and the junior salesman wanted help talking him into a purchase. Evan adjusted his tie and walked over. Antonio might have a crisis with his youngest daughter, but as far as Evan knew, it wasn't life and death. Business came first. It was life.

Forty minutes later, Evan wheeled out of the parking lot and headed toward the other side of town. A cash down payment was in the safe, but it had taken longer than expected. At the Berzani homestead, he parked on the street and headed up the walk. As he had for nearly twenty years, he knocked once and let himself in.

The interior of the house was cool, dim and quiet. No one was in the living room off to the left of the entry hall. As always, there was a fabulous aroma coming from the kitchen. Oregano, sage, basil: the herbs filled the house. And though he was not born a Berzani, they smelled like home.

Evan followed his nose down the hall to the back of

the house. As he passed the staircase he ran a hand over the newel post. For an instant, he thought he saw a girl descending from the second floor. It was Anna—a younger version. She wore a bikini covered by a red, tiny excuse for a skirt. She was going for a swim or something. A yellow-and-turquoise beach towel was draped over one shoulder, sunglasses perched on top of her head. It was a vision from many years ago, a moment he had forgotten. Except some demon in his head had decided to dig it up to torment him.

This had to stop, but how? Time, he told himself, it would take time. He had ridden this roller coaster before; somehow, he had survived those early years and he would again. Shaking his head, he passed the dining room, the setting for so many family meals he had shared with Anna and the whole Berzani clan. It was quiet. Strangely, there weren't any sounds coming from the other side of the kitchen door, either. He pushed through and stopped abruptly. The three men sitting at the kitchen table turned to look his way as if pulled on strings.

"Sorry I'm late." Evan's heart began to pound when no one said anything. "What's wrong?"

ANNA SAT IN THE CAR FOR a moment after pulling into her parents' driveway. A soft, sweet-smelling breeze wafted in the open window and flirted with her hair, twirling tendrils across her cheeks. Worries also swirled around inside her head: Where was Evan? What was he doing? Were his parents okay?

And the biggest of all: How was she going to tell him she was pregnant?

In a burst of frustration, she closed the windows, turned off the engine and got out of the car. What a wasted afternoon. After seeing Mimi, she had gone in search of Evan, only to be stymied. At the car dealership, a salesman had said he was out on a family emergency. He had given her Evan's card with his cell phone number, but she had been reluctant to call. If there was trouble with his father or mother, it was no time to disturb him with her news.

After staring at the small white rectangle for fifteen minutes, she had finally dialed the number. She got his voice mail, cursed modern technology, then left a message. She hoped her tone was noncommittal, telling him only that she needed to see him soon. Now she could do nothing but wait for him to contact her.

Inside the house, Anna headed for the stairs, hoping to avoid her father and mother. But as she put one foot on the bottom step, she heard her father's raised voice coming from the kitchen. She was two steps up when she heard him say her name. She froze. He was yelling something about *her*. It didn't take a genius to figure out why.

Anna sighed. She had no choice: she had to face him, if only for damage control. If she avoided it, she would feel— and act—like a coward. She had nothing to be ashamed of, she told herself. This pregnancy was a surprise, but it wasn't a scandal. She wasn't going to let her father turn it into one, either.

Leaving her purse on the steps, she squared her shoulders and went down the hall. Taking a deep breath, Anna held it, let it release slowly, then pushed through the swinging door into the kitchen.

"Because it is *our* name, *our* reputation," Antonio shouted. His hands were in the air, punctuating his words with a wide, sweeping gesture. His disputant was his wife, who stood facing him, irritation clearly evident on her face.

Behind Elaine, Anna saw Patrick and Ian leaning against the counter next to the sink. They were both somber and quiet, which was unusual. Antonio and Elaine's fights were legendary and always entertaining. Her brothers usually egged them on, grinning as the volume increased.

"What has been done to my child, my baby, *must* be paid for." Her father waved a hand at Anna as he spoke. "Whoever has done this will answer!"

"She is my child, too." Elaine's voice rose to a crescendo. "And this is *not* Sicily!"

"Wait a minute here—" Anna began.

"Ask him." Antonio pointed across the room. "I am sure he agrees with me. Tell them, Evan, what a man must do."

Feeling as though she was in one of those nightmares where she couldn't move fast enough to save herself, Anna turned her head. Evan sat barely three feet from her, in a chair at the head of the table. Their eyes met, his a blazing green. Anna swallowed on a completely dry throat. So this was the family emergency. Not his family, but *hers*. Her lips parted, but no words would come out. What could she say, anyway? The horrified panic in his eyes, his face as white as porcelain, told her everything.

Evan *knew*.

A terror flooded through Anna, making her shake. Even though she had been bracing herself for the worst, somehow she hadn't understood just how awful this moment would be. Part of her had gripped tightly to the fantasy of his excitement, his joy.

But Evan was *not* going to be excited. He was *not* going to hold her and tell her he was happy. He was *not* going to proclaim his love for her and the child they had created. And worst of all, since Antonio was still on a manhunt, Evan had obviously not told anyone that he was the father-to-be.

Anna felt a wash of dizziness. The room started to lose

color. The lights seemed to dim. The cabinets on the walls slid away from her at an alarming speed. She swayed.

I'm fainting, she told herself. It was a calming thought. Oblivion offered sanctuary. She welcomed the descending blackness like a friend as her mind went blank. But this new friend didn't take her far. She could still hear a shout, feel strong arms close around her body. Her cheek rested gratefully on a close, convenient shoulder. A citrus tang filled her nostrils.

"Here, let me," a man said. His voice was far away at first, then came closer.

"Watch out. I've got her," a second man said right next to her ear, his voice a snap of irritation.

How nice to be fought over, Anna thought idly as she drifted just beneath the surface of consciousness. Arms cradled her, kept her safe. Her eyelids fluttered open as her body was lowered onto soft cushions. She saw Evan's face inches from hers. His eyes had darkened to jade and were filled with worry. *Poor Evan.* She wanted to comfort him or invite him to join her in her peaceful floating, but couldn't. She closed her eyes again.

"Here," she heard her mother say. "Make her take a sip of this."

Anna was pulled upright and a splash of strongly alcoholic liquid filled her mouth. Her eyelids flew open as she swallowed, then choked and coughed. "Ugh! That's awful."

"Lie down again," Evan told her. His hands pressed gently on her shoulders. "Give it a minute."

Slowly, Anna realized she had traveled only as far as the living room sofa. Evan must have carried her. He was kneeling beside her, while Ian bent over the back cushions, peering at her. Her father was pacing back and forth.

"Sorry," she said softly. Evan remained silent. His lashes

lowered over his eyes, the thick blond fringe hiding their expression. He seemed to hesitate, then stood and backed away to let Elaine minister to her daughter.

Sitting up, Anna waved away her mother's attempts to pile pillows around her. "I'm okay, Ma. Really."

"You should rest a—"

"I was just dizzy, that's all."

Elaine brushed the hair from her face with a gentle touch. "Are you sure?"

"See! Keeping her secret has made her sick." Antonio sat in a chair opposite the sofa and put his hands on his knees, his eyes locked on his daughter. "We must know, Anna Maria. Who did this to you?"

"Antonio! This is not the time for an inquisition," Elaine insisted.

"Pop, I told you this morning, no one *did* this to me." Anna swung her feet to the floor. Luckily there was no nausea or vertigo this time. She darted a quick glance at Evan who stood with his hands in his pockets, his eyes on the floor. Instinctively, she knew there would be no help from him.

"It takes two to tango," Patrick said from somewhere behind her.

"Thank you, Dr. Phil." Anna looked at her brother with annoyance. "But until I talk to my *dance partner,* his identity is none of your business."

"It is, if this guy's not going to step up to the plate."

"Who said he wasn't?" Anna demanded. "I haven't even told him, Patty. How do you know what he will or won't do?"

"He'd better do the right thing," Patrick said fiercely. "Or he'll have me to answer to."

Anna swiveled around to glare at him again. She wondered if he would say the same thing when she told him it was his best friend doing the dancing. "This is ridiculous," she muttered, rubbing a hand across her forehead.

"We just want to help," Ian said softly.

"Then leave it alone," she said with a snap. Anna closed her eyes. What a surreal moment: here was her family, threatening the father of her baby while the man stood right in the room. Stood *silently* in the room, her aching heart noted, while she, all alone, defended his reputation.

Anna opened her eyes and turned to glare at Evan. He was stationed near the bookcase, but was now watching her warily. "What about you, McKenzie?" she asked abruptly. "Do you think the guy should be strung up?"

He jerked slightly, shifting from one foot to the other. "It…depends on what he does when he finds out."

"So, what do you think he'll do when I tell him?" Anna stared hard at Evan. "Do you think he'll do the *right* thing?"

"Whatever that is." Evan gave an awkward shrug of his shoulders, then glared back at her, his expression hard. "He deserves a chance to think about it. You can't just spring it on the poor bastard and expect him to act like a prince."

"Don't ask McKenzie about this," Patrick interrupted impatiently. "He hasn't got the first clue about kids or marriage."

Anna bit her tongue. She wanted to scream the truth, but one thing held her back: Evan's continued silence. It spoke too loudly for him. He was clearly embarrassed to be here. Anna wondered if he was ashamed of himself. Then it struck her that he could be ashamed of her—*and* their baby. That was the worst thought of all.

She stood up, not dizzy at all now, and looked at her family. "Look, I appreciate the fact that you're concerned for me. But I need some time to sort things out. I'm still in a state of shock. I guess we all are. When I need something I'll let you know."

Everyone stayed where they were, remaining silent as she turned and walked out of the room. When she passed Evan, she looked at him, giving him one last chance, but his face was blank. She brushed past him and fled up the stairs, carrying a new life in her womb and an unbearable pain in her heart.

Chapter Seven

The slam of Anna's door seemed to reanimate those she had left behind in the living room. Antonio slapped his knees and sat back in his chair with a huff. Patrick came around the sofa and dropped down next to his mother. Ian stayed where he was, leaning against the door frame, arms crossed over his chest, face inscrutable.

Evan didn't move, either. He had become frozen, like one of the bookends on the shelves next to him. Anna's last look of scorn had etched his soul with fire and condemned it to suffer.

What did she expect of him? What was he supposed to say, here in front of her parents, her brothers, his best friend? It was his family, too. The more he thought of it, the more irritated he became. Raising a hand, he raked his fingers through his hair. The gesture brought everyone's attention to him.

"So, you have an idea for us?" Antonio asked. His tone was almost belligerent. "A plan? How do we find this *culo* who has done this thing to my daughter."

"No. I just…uh…" Evan stopped and shook his head. He tried not to squirm. The urge to confess was overwhelming, but he clenched his teeth and held it back. Sooner or later, they would have to know. He would *have* to tell them, but not yet—not until he talked to Anna. "She needs time," he continued lamely.

"Evan is right," Elaine said softly. "We *all* need time. We must be patient. No one should badger Anna about who the father is."

"But—"

"No one," she said, interrupting Patrick. Antonio was silent, but Evan could see the stubborn glint in the older man's eyes. Elaine obviously saw it, too, for she leveled a stern gaze at her husband. They both stared at each other, as if daring the other to speak first.

"So what are we having for dinner?" Ian finally asked no one in particular.

"Oh, I forgot the beans in the oven!" Elaine rose and dashed from the room.

"Pop, you got enough beer?" Patrick asked, rising to his feet.

"I am out of Yuengling," Antonio answered.

"I have to go pick up Kate and Beth. I'll get some on my way back."

"And get Peroni, as well."

Everyone slowly dispersed. Evan was unsurprised that the latest family disaster had not postponed the barbeque. The Berzanis would never let a little thing like a surprise pregnancy get in the way of food. He cringed to think that he would be expected to be there. He followed Patrick and Ian out of the house and fell into step beside them. They reached the curb and Evan punched the unlock button on his key fob.

"I guess I'll see you tonight," he said.

"If I have to be here, so do you," Ian said. "We have to keep Pop from cornering Anna."

"What about stopping *me?* I'm on Pop's side," Patrick said.

"That's funny," Ian said, looking over at his brother. "Weren't you the one who knocked up some girl recently?"

"It wasn't like that and you know it. But if this guy—"

"Stuff it," Ian said with a snort. "He's three-thousand miles away, safe and sound in the big state of California."

"Well, if I find him, I'll teach him how to keep his zipper zipped," Patrick said darkly.

"Ian's right. Don't be such a hypocrite," Evan said with a snap. "You were in the exact same spot once upon a time. Nobody was tracking you down and—"

"Hey, pal, I *married* the mother of my child," Patrick said, thumping a finger on his chest.

"Really? I thought you married Kate because you loved her," Ian said mildly.

"Oh, shut up," Patrick said.

"Maybe Anna doesn't want to get married. Have you thought of that?" Evan asked. "Or maybe this guy's an asshole and she *shouldn't* marry him? And why is marriage the only answer, anyway?"

"It's not the *only* answer, but I'm not going to stand by and let some guy use my sister and walk away whistling." They glared at each other, then Patrick asked, "What's got *you* so worked up? You should be on my side."

Evan backpedaled hastily. "I just don't think you should jump to conclusions."

"You know McKenzie's philosophically opposed to marriage, Patty," Ian said, looking at Evan. "He wouldn't wish it on his worst enemy."

Patrick grinned suddenly. "Oh, he'll change his mind eventually."

"Not in this lifetime," Evan said, completely serious. He

shifted his shoulders, uncomfortable with the conversation. "I've got to go change out of this suit. Later."

He turned and got into his car without another word. He revved the engine and kicked it into First. Glancing in his rearview mirror, he saw the other two men still standing on the sidewalk, watching his departure. A shiver crept over Evan's skin and an invisible hand twisted his gut.

What a mess.

Rounding the corner, he blended into the rush-hour traffic. Driving through town on autopilot, Evan's mind was whirling, but he couldn't make sense of anything. Shock had set in as soon as Antonio had used the words *Anna* and *pregnant* in the same sentence. He hadn't shaken it off since. While the Berzanis had discussed preserving family honor, the decadent state of modern love and how to track down the perpetrator, he had sat in stunned silence. One word had reverberated in his brain like a drumbeat: no.

No.

No.

Then Anna had walked into the kitchen and his world had spun completely off its axis. He knew the truth when their eyes met. The night he had been trying so hard to forget would *never* be forgotten.

Evan parked in front of his condo and got out of the car. Trudging up the stairs to the front door, he pulled out his cell phone. Scrolling through the missed calls, his steps slowed when he saw Anna's number. He let himself in the house as he punched the buttons to hear the messages. He stopped dead when Anna's voice filled his ear.

"Hi, it's Anna. I need to talk to you…to see you…as soon as possible. Please call me when you get this." The message clicked off and he slowly closed the door behind him. Yeah, she had needed to see him all right, except he was sure he had seen more than enough of her.

Evan pulled off his jacket and draped it over the back of a chair. Loosening his tie, he went to the kitchen and pulled out a bottle of Scotch. Pouring a generous shot in a glass, he tossed back the fiery liquid and poured another. Resting his forehead against an upper cabinet, he closed his eyes.

Unbidden, the image of Anna, pale and limp in his arms, rose in his mind's eye. She had scared the shit out of him when her eyes rolled up in her head. Without even thinking, he had lunged, catching her as she crumpled. Even now, the image conjured another wave of sheer panic and his pulse quickened. Holding her, protecting her, was all that mattered in that instant, but he had felt completely helpless, too. She had been so light and fragile in his arms, looked so small. Vulnerable. And he could do nothing but carry her to the sofa.

He pushed away from the cabinet and went into the living room, carrying his glass with him. The memory and the feelings followed, keeping him unsettled. He wondered how she was feeling now. Was she sick? Dizzy? She was definitely angry. He had seen that clearly enough. Pressing two fingers into his eye sockets, he tried to force back the thoughts, but they wouldn't obey. What she was feeling didn't matter.

Except that it did.

Putting down his drink, Evan grabbed his phone again. He couldn't put off talking to her. At the least, they needed to come up with some plan of defense before the barbeque tonight.

The phone rang once, then twice. "Hello?"

"It's Evan." Silence answered him. Pacing to the window, he leaned against the sill. "Anna?"

"What do you want?" Her tone was subzero.

He bristled. His earlier concern for her well-being disappeared in a heartbeat. "What do *I* want? I want you to tell me to wake up from this nightmare."

"You think I don't want that, too?" Anna's voice was furious now.

"What the hell happened? I thought you were on the pill."

"*I am!*" Anna yelled. "How was I supposed to know that having the flu would mess things up? Do you think I planned this? That I *wanted* to have your child?"

"I haven't known *what* to think since your dad hit me with this. Why didn't you tell me first?" he demanded.

"I tried to!"

"Not very damned hard," he said in a growl.

"I went to the dealership, Evan," Anna said, her voice dropping to match his low, angry tone. "I left a message for you. What else was I supposed to do? I didn't know Pop would go on the rampage like this."

"Well, if you were around a little more, you'd remember what he's like." Evan combed a hand through his hair and gripped the back of his neck. He groaned. "Dammit, Anna, he's going to kill me. Your mother's going to do something worse! What the hell am I supposed to do?"

"How or what you tell my parents is the least of *my* worries," Anna said coldly. "Have you forgotten that I'm the one that's pregnant?"

"I wish I could." He muttered the words under his breath, but she obviously heard them.

"Is it possible for you to stop thinking about yourself for a minute?" Her voice rose again.

Evan bit back the callous words that leaped to his tongue. This sniping was getting them nowhere. What they needed was to step back and figure out what deal they could strike. There had to be a compromise to satisfy them both—happy was too much to ask for.

"Look. We've got to talk."

"Sure," Anna said sarcastically. "Before or after my father serves up the spareribs?"

"Not tonight." The possibility of having this conversation around her family made his palms sweat. Evan rubbed a hand over his face. "Let's just get through the meal. We'll meet tomorrow and…and figure out what to do."

"Great," she said sourly. "I'll look forward to it."

"All right. Where do you—" He stopped abruptly, realizing that she had hung up on him.

Pulling the phone away from his ear, he stared at it. A red haze of anger surged through him. He threw the phone across the room with all his might. It hit the far wall, just below a photo of the Chesapeake Bay Bridge, and exploded into plastic bits that flew off in all directions. Not bothering to check the damage to the wall or his phone, Evan stalked over to the sofa and dropped down onto it. He put his hands over his face and swore in a soft, steady stream.

What the hell was he going to do now?

POINTING HER CAMERA AT the supply shed, Anna checked the viewfinder and let the autofocus do its job. A pause, a click and the image flashed on the screen. Checking it, she decided it would do. Rotating a few degrees, she took another shot and then another, until she had the entire west side of the boatyard captured in pixels. Later, she could stitch them together for a full panorama on her computer. Taking out a small voice recorder, she began dictating notes on the site details.

The routine of working a prospective site—measuring, recording, photographing—calmed Anna. It was a welcome respite from the jolts and surprises she had experienced since arriving in Crab Creek two days ago. The complications and turmoil would no doubt return soon, but for now she was simply Anna Berzani, architect. That's all she wanted to be for as long as possible.

Pacing off an area near the wood shop, Anna sketched some details on the old site plan that her father had given her. Over twenty-five years old, not much had changed since the original layout, just two new boat sheds and an addition to the paint shop. She could gauge the approximate property lines from the buildings and fences. Later, she would have a surveyor verify that all this dirt really belonged to her parents.

Anna edged her way behind the shop, through a tangle of rusty jack stands and the chain-link fence. A wild-rose bramble creeping through the fence caught at her jeans. She unhooked the thorn and let it spring back out of the way. When she reached the corner of the fence, she sighted down to the water, then turned ninety degrees and looked up toward the front gate. Both fence runs looked pretty straight-line and matched the plan.

Continuing around the building, Anna recorded more observations. Cobwebs clung to her shoulder and neck, irritating her. Brushing them aside, her hand left a streak of dirt on her pale blue T-shirt. A curl of hair worked itself out of her ponytail and she tucked it behind one ear. She was getting dirty, disheveled and sweaty poking around in forgotten corners of the yard, but she promised herself a large bottle of ice-cold water when she finished.

Ideas flashed through her head of what she would design: condos, a restaurant, shops. The site was wider than it was deep, with a long water frontage. The view would be the main feature of any building she created, overlooking the boats and, beyond that, the ever-changing waters of the Chesapeake. Of course the marina would stay. Everyone agreed about that. And about a restaurant: a nice seafood place with a deck. In good weather, folks would flock to it by land and sea.

Picking her way past a pile of lumber, Anna emerged from the shadows of the wood shop, into the dazzling sunlight, and reached for her sunglasses.

"Hey."

The greeting was so startling, so unexpected and so close that Anna's tape measure, sunglasses, clipboard and the site plan clattered to the ground. She only just managed to save her camera from taking the same tumble. Whirling around, she saw Evan standing a few feet away.

"You scared the bejesus out of me!" she said. As she collected her tools, she kept her face averted, not wanting to reveal how flustered she felt or how hard the blood pulsed through her veins.

Evan grabbed the site plan before the wind blew it away. "Sorry, I thought you saw me." He looked at the drawing in his hand. "What are you doing?"

"My job," she replied coolly. "What are *you* doing?"

"Looking for you." His eyes were bloodshot with dark circles under them. He must have slept worse than she had last night. For a moment, Anna almost felt sorry for him. He wore faded jeans, a wrinkled T-shirt that looked slept-in and tennis shoes. Though it was far from his usual elegant attire, he somehow managed to make himself look gorgeous. "We have to talk, Anna."

Biting her lip, she nodded. They had deliberately steered clear of each other at the barbeque, circling opposite sides of the patio, while trying not to appear too obvious about it. But dodging each other solved nothing. She glanced around the yard. A few workers were at the travel lift, hoisting an old ketch out of the water. Patrick or her father could not be far away.

"Not here."

Evan nodded and turned without a word. He led the way to a dark blue sedan and opened the door for her. She balked and brushed at the dirt and cobwebs on her T-shirt again. "I should go home and change."

"Doesn't matter," he said, shaking his head.

"I might dirty the upholstery."

"It's mine. Get in."

Anna slid into the passenger seat as ordered. Evan came around to the other side, started the engine and backed out of the parking spot.

"I thought you only drove sporty convertibles."

"Meaning what? I'm all flash and no substance?" He had slipped on sunglasses, and she couldn't read his expression. He let out a humorless laugh. "Isn't this a better image for an expectant father?"

Looking at her hands knotted together in her lap, Anna couldn't think of a neutral reply to this. They traveled in silence until he pulled up in front of a small coffee shop two blocks off Main Street. She got out before he could come around, but he closed the door for her, then ushered her inside.

They stepped up to the counter and ordered drinks from a barrista who might be male or female. Anna wasn't quite sure. He or she ignored Anna and flirted unabashedly with Evan, greeting him by name. The place reminded her of a coffee shop on Geary that she frequented in San Francisco. She felt a pang of homesickness and wished she was there now.

"You apparently come here often," she observed as they took their drinks and sat at a table in the back.

"I suppose I do. I sold the owner a delivery van a few years ago. We're not likely to see anyone we know here."

Anna took a drink of her iced herbal tea. Evan leaned forward, elbows on the table, his eyes on the coffee cup in front of him. Spinning her glass one way, then another, Anna fumbled for a way to begin.

"So, I was thinking—"

"I had a—"

They both spoke and stopped at once.

"You go first," she told Evan.

"All right." He cleared his throat, looking at her with wary eyes. "I thought about this all night. First, don't take this the wrong way, but you're keeping the kid, right?"

Anna wondered how she could take the question the *right* way. The distance it put between them yawned like a chasm. If she hadn't known Evan was unhappy about the fix they were in, this proved it. Her heart ached and her stomach clenched in sympathetic pain. She nodded in answer, unable to speak.

"I figured." Evan sipped his coffee. "So. You'll need money to do this right and I—"

"I have money, Evan." Anger helped Anna find her voice. "A home, too, and a good job with benefits."

"Yeah, but you won't be able to work for a while. When you do go back, the kid's going to need a nanny or day care, something like that. I can set up a trust fund. That way you won't have to worry about expenses and when college comes around—"

"I'm three *weeks* pregnant, Evan. I don't think we need to worry about college yet."

"Well, you'll be alone and I just thought that..." His voice trailed off as he looked at her. "I mean, you'll be in California and I'll be here."

"I'm thinking about moving back," she said, watching him closely.

He blinked once and took a drink of his coffee before replying in an even tone, "That makes sense. Your mother will love it. Pop, too. And I'll be around to help as much as I can."

She stared at him, eyes narrowed. "That sounds almost like being a father."

"I *am* the father," Evan said.

"Is this how a real father acts? Funny, I thought there'd be more of a celebration. Cigars, maybe." Anna shook her head. "All I've seen is you pretending you're not involved."

"You think I want to deceive your family like this? If I knew a clean way out, I'd take it in a heartbeat," he said in an irritated snap. His eyes smoldered with frustration.

Now she was getting a reaction, one that shook her. Her fingers clenched on her cup, then she pointed to the door. "So, there's the way out. Take it."

Evan sat back. Raking a hand through his hair, his fingers ruffled the blond strands, leaving some of them sticking straight up. He looked as though he was on the verge of taking her offer and walking away.

"I take full responsibility for what happened, Annie." He met her gaze with his own, the anger in his voice tightly reined. "We can do joint parenting, partial custody, whatever. My dad had me part-time after the divorce, so I know the basic rules of the game."

"There are rules? Like what?" she asked sourly. "You get weekend outings and I take the day-to-day child rearing?"

"No. It wouldn't be like that." He leaned forward again and lowered his voice. "I'll support you however you want and give you whatever you need."

The conversation felt surreal. It was not at all what she had expected, or hoped. But why should she be surprised? When had Evan McKenzie said or done what anyone expected? She pushed her tea to one side, laying her hands flat on the table. The wood was rough under her fingertips, scarred by carvings through layers of varnish.

"Whatever I need," Anna repeated. She held his gaze with her own.

"Anything. Just ask."

"Would you marry me?"

Evan stared back at her. She saw first confusion, then surprise, then something that came close to disgust. He shook his head. "No. Anything but that."

Anna nodded, not surprised. Still, she lowered her head, blinking back tears that threatened. When she had herself under control, she looked into his eyes, bright green against pale skin. Her gaze traced his face. She was reminded how he appeared yesterday in her parents' kitchen: a hunted animal, trapped, cornered, ready to bite and claw to defend itself.

"Then I don't need anything from you, Evan," she said softly.

"What are we going to tell your parents?"

As painful as it was, his question told her where his principal concerns lay. "I'll tell them that this child is mine and I'll raise it on my own. Don't worry. It's our secret. Something we'll share forever."

With that, she stood and walked out of the coffee shop. Outside in the sunlight, she suddenly realized she had come here in Evan's car and had no transportation back. She didn't turn around, didn't ask for his aid. She was alone now. She had better start getting used to it.

Chapter Eight

Rain streaked the huge plate-glass showroom windows. A tropical depression had drifted northward and hung over the mid-Atlantic region, drenching it. Southerly winds were pushing the waters of the Chesapeake up to meet swollen rivers and streams. Flash-flood warnings were posted for parts of the northern counties. The dismal weather perfectly echoed Evan's mood. Both had stunk since Anna's departure one week ago.

The showroom was quiet and the car lot deserted. Brett, the only other person there, manned a desk, on the remote chance that a customer would appear, or at least call. Evan bet no one would show up this afternoon.

"You don't have to stick around," Evan said, turning his head toward the other man. "This rain's going to kill business. We'll hope it lets up this weekend."

"I'm just catching up on paperwork," Brett said. "Besides, if I go home, my wife'll be on me."

"Trouble in paradise?"

"The usual," the other man said with a shrug. "'Honey, do this,' 'honey, do that.'"

"The *usual*." Evan muttered the words to himself as he turned back to watch the rain streak down the windows.

How many times had he heard just that phrase—or worse—from his married friends and acquaintances? How many people were just marking time in their relationships, feeling stuck, but unable to break free? Or were they simply unwilling? Maybe it was lethargy or ignorance. He didn't know, but he knew he didn't want the same for himself. He also knew marrying Anna for the sake of their child was the worst thing he could do. He would feel trapped, forever trying to escape. Just like his father.

He wished some prospect would show up to look at a car. Even a tire-kicking time-waster asking innumerable idiotic questions with no intention of buying a car would be welcome right now. He considered letting Brett cover the floor, but what would Evan do then? Sailing was out, so was running or biking. He could sit at home and let the walls close in, but that wasn't any different from what he was doing here. At least the showroom had volume; it took a while for claustrophobia to set in—or whatever it was he was feeling.

As he brooded, a car pulled up outside. Headlights flashed through the mist, briefly sparkling across the cars parked inside the showroom. Finally, some distraction from the tumult inside his own head. Pulling his hands from his pockets, Evan absently straightened his tie. The driver stepped out of his car and made a quick dash for the portico over the double doors. The prospect had his hood up against the rain, but it was a man, older. Judging by the cut of his clothes, he probably had money, but not loaded. Of course you could never tell. Evan had learned that.

Evan noticed that Brett had perked up, as well. He had risen from his desk and slipped on his jacket, ready for action. With a wave of his hand, Evan motioned to him. Brett grinned and sat down again, pretending to be busy with some contract. The signal was simple: *let him come to us.* Bad enough that they were bored, there was no need to let the customer know that, too.

The red raincoat came through the door. A large hand brushed back the hood. The welcoming smile on Evan's face faded as Antonio Berzani revealed himself. What had brought him out on such a miserable day? Was it Anna? The baby? Had she finally told Antonio who had fathered her child? Since Anna's departure, Evan hadn't seen Antonio or any of the Berzanis. After all these years of finding a second home with them, that security was gone. He couldn't tell him what he had done. He couldn't hurt them that way. Nor could he bear losing their love. So he had steered clear of them. Now, seeing Antonio, a wave of dread washed over Evan.

Surreptitiously, he wiped his sweating palms against his trousers and put on his game face. "Pop! What brings you out in this weather?"

"I need to speak with you," Antonio said, solemnly clasping Evan's hand and squeezing it firmly. His dark eyes held a message Evan couldn't interpret. "About Anna."

A line of sweat popped out on Evan's forehead. He had avoided divulging the truth for too long. Now it had come calling at his door. "Ah…sure. Let's go in my office. Brett, take the floor."

Brett buttoned his jacket and replaced Evan at his post by the window. In his private office, Evan took Antonio's coat as the older man shrugged it off. He hung it behind the door.

"Can I get you some coffee?"

"No. Nothing for me."

Antonio plopped into one of the cushy chairs before the desk. Evan sat behind it. His stomach was in knots, but he tried to act brave. "What's this about Anna, Pop?"

"I cannot let this endure another minute." Antonio banged a fist on Evan's desk. "I must have the truth!"

Evan nearly jumped out of his chair. "I was going to tell—"

"So you *do* know!" Antonio interrupted triumphantly.

"Well, ah…" Evan fumbled to a halt.

His brain caught up with his panic, slowing his confession. Why wasn't Antonio coming across the desk at him? He should be furious, at the least. But his face wore a look of zealous inquiry, not wrath. Evan stared at the older man as a rush of giddy relief flooded through him: Antonio did not know the truth after all.

Antonio hardly noticed Evan's stammered reply. "Tell me the name of this scoundrel," he demanded, shaking a finger at Evan. "He *must* fulfill his duty to my daughter."

Evan scrambled for a way to back out. "I just…well… Let's just say I have a suspect in mind. But I…I don't want to accuse an innocent man."

Antonio scowled at this. "It does not matter. The name of a dishonorable man is worthless anyway. But he is in San Francisco?"

"He *was*," Evan felt obligated to say.

"I knew it!"

"Hold on a second, Pop. Last time I spoke with Anna, she had decided to raise the baby on her own."

"That is what she *thinks*." Antonio tapped a finger to his forehead, his dark eyes glittering. "*We* are going to change her mind."

"We are?"

"Yes. We are going to San Francisco—"

Evan sat up straight. "Us? Wait a minute—"

"—and restore my daughter's honor."

"But how—"

Antonio shrugged, as if a particular strategy mattered little. "We will talk to her. You have a rapport with Anna."

"No, I don't. We fight constantly."

"True, you and she have always squabbled. It is natural, like a brother and sister. But the day we discussed developing the marina, the ideas flew from the two of you. First one, then the other, as if you were one mind." Antonio pointed a finger at Evan. "It was *clear.* You understand her as no one else does. I considered asking Patrick or Ian, but I have thought it through carefully. *You* are the one who must go."

Evan pressed a hand to the top of his head, feeling as if it was going to blow off. This was the most ridiculous conversation he had ever had. Brother and *sister?* If Antonio only knew. He had to squelch this immediately.

"Listen, Pop. I know that Anna's decision has upset you, but it's *her* decision." He leaned forward, resting his elbows on the desk. "We can only give her whatever help she asks for."

"No," Antonio said calmly. "My Anna is a strong woman. Her mother and I raised her to be so. But she is not in her right mind. Raising a child is not something you do alone." He held up a hand to stop Evan from protesting. "I know there are many women who do this, but that does not make it right. And besides, they have families to help them. Anna has no one in that city."

"She has friends," Evan said lamely.

"It is not the same. Anna chooses to live far away from us. I do not like it, but I cannot force her to return," Antonio said, sitting back in his chair. "So, I must be sure that the father of her child will support her. This nameless man has a responsibility. He will answer for that."

Staring at the older man, Evan groped for a counter-argument, but there was none to be found. Antonio was right: the father *should* support Anna and her baby. They needed him, whether she—or he—realized it or not. The past week of restless nights and distracted days had taught him that much.

With a gusted sigh, Evan sat back in his chair. "Okay. I'll go see her."

"*We* will go see her."

"Pop, I think it's best if I go alone. I can—"

"I am her father," Antonio said firmly. "She still has some respect for me."

"You two in the same room, Pop, sometimes that's not such a smart thing," Evan suggested.

"This is true. And it is why I will give you time alone with her."

Evan knew he was beat. For now, at least. Maybe Elaine could hold Antonio safe at home. "I'll look into tickets, then."

"No need. I have already bought them. We leave tomorrow morning." Antonio stood and went to the coatrack. He pulled out a piece of paper from an inside pocket in his jacket and brought it to Evan. "And we are in luck! I have a cousin there. He owns a restaurant in a section called North Beach. The best Italian food in the city. I have spoken to him and all is arranged. He promises to prepare us a feast to remember."

Evan suppressed the urge to pound his forehead on the desk. Instead, he took the e-ticket, perused it and set it aside. It seemed he was stuck. The best he could hope for was to keep Antonio on a tight rein and get him there and back with the least collateral damage.

"I guess I'll pick you up in the morning," Evan said, completely defeated. He came around the desk to help Antonio back into his coat.

"You are a good son, Evan. Sometimes better than my own." Antonio had a broad grin on his face. "But better not mention that to Ian and Patricio." He reached out and embraced Evan heartily, pounding him on the back. "We will save Anna and she will be grateful. You will see."

Evan hugged the man back, but he could only imitate the enthusiasm halfheartedly. Antonio's praise was like salt in a wound: in truth, he was the worst son imaginable. The hole he was digging for himself was getting deeper and deeper by the day, too, and telling Antonio the truth seemed more impossible than ever.

HOURS LATER, EVAN SAT on his sofa with a sigh. He was exhausted. After Antonio had gone, Evan had left the showroom in Brett's capable hands and fled to the gym. He hated working out inside a building, but forced himself through a session with weights and five miles on the treadmill, just to clear his mind. With music blasting in his ears, and his blood pumping, he was able to tune out the world and—most important—his own thoughts.

At home, he took a shower and packed for his flight. It was only overnight, so he didn't need much. Memories of his last trip to San Francisco tried to creep into his head, but he resolutely forced them back. This journey would be completely different. He fixed an easy meal of pasta and salad, then took a glass of wine into the living room and turned on the television. Preseason football was on—the Ravens versus the Redskins—and he watched the game as a diversion.

The distraction wasn't working too well when his doorbell rang in the second quarter. Evan was glad for the interruption, but not so eager to entertain surprise visitors. He turned off the television, got up and went down the hall to the door. Ian stood there.

"What do you want?" Evan asked.

"That's a charming greeting," Ian said with a grin.

When Evan didn't move, he added, "Are you going to ask me in?"

Evan grunted and stood back, then closed the door behind his friend.

"Man, it's a wet one out there," Ian said, shucking his raincoat.

"But you came out anyway," Even said, eyeing the other man guardedly. "I've got a bottle of red open, or there's a beer in the fridge."

"Wine's great, thanks."

Evan went into the kitchen, grabbed a glass and the bottle, bringing both to the living room where Ian had seated himself on the leather love seat perpendicular to the sofa. He poured the cabernet and topped his own glass before setting the bottle on the coffee table. Sitting in his spot on the sofa again, he raised his glass and said, "Cheers."

Ian lifted his glass in return and sipped. He pursed his lips appreciatively. "You've got faults, McKenzie, but picking a bad wine isn't one of them. I wish you'd stock Pop's cellar. That Italian *rustico* crap he's been buying lately is awful."

"Is that why you're here? A wine tasting?" Evan asked, raising an eyebrow.

"Nope." Ian sipped again. "Rumor around the homestead says you're going to San Fran with Pop tomorrow."

Evan sank back into the cushions. "That's the plan."

Ian nodded. "I hear one of you is twisting Anna's arm until she reveals who the father is."

"Ask Pop about that."

"I did." Ian gazed over at him for a minute, his dark eyes unreadable. "Now I'm asking you. Since Pop says *you* know who it is."

A prickle of fear crept up Evan's spine. Ian would not be so easy to waylay as Antonio. "I never said that."

"He's got a different story." Ian leaned forward and set his glass on the coffee table. He clasped his hands together in front of him. "When were you going to admit it, Evan?"

Ian's voice was quiet and held no anger, but there was a thread of steel in it that Evan had heard maybe twice in his life. The other Berzanis were volatile, erupting at a moment's notice, but not Ian. His anger was controlled and very deliberate. Evan sensed that it was about to be unleashed on him.

"Anna doesn't want anyone to know," he said softly.

"*Anna* doesn't?" The steel grew harder. "What the hell does *that* matter? You knock my sister up and don't own up to it? Excuse me, but I've got a problem with that."

"You think I meant to do this?" Evan set his glass down with a crack, ignoring the wine that sloshed out on the table. He got to his feet, unable to stay still. "It was an accident! She was on the pill and it didn't work and—"

He stopped in front of the window, putting his hands over his face before running them back into his hair. The night outside the windows was dark and featureless, the usual view out onto the Chesapeake Bay shrouded by rain. Behind him, Ian didn't make a sound. Evan wished he could turn and find the man gone. He didn't want to see the anger and loathing sure to be on his friend's face.

Swallowing, Evan turned anyway. "I didn't want any of this. It just…happened."

As Ian stared at him, his eyes narrowed. "So what are you going to do about it?"

"I honestly don't know," Evan said, shoving his hands in his pockets. He leaned back against the cold glass. "I tried to talk to her, but…"

"But what?"

"She doesn't want my money and she doesn't want my help."

"Then what *does* she want?" Ian asked.

Evan looked down at the floor. "She asked me if I'd marry her," he said quietly.

"And?"

"I said no."

Ian was silent. Evan heard him pick up his glass and drink, then set it down again. Evan lifted his head and looked over at the other man. "It would be a mistake, Ian. I don't love her and—"

"Then why'd you screw her?" Ian interrupted with a snap. "She's not just some woman you pick up and drop, McKenzie. This is my *sister* we're talking about. Hell, she's practically *your* sister."

It was Evan's turn to remain silent. Ian was right and there was nothing he could say to defend himself. Ian rose and began to pace the room between the windows and the bar separating the kitchen from the rest of the space.

"Look," he said, coming to a stop in front of Evan. "All those years, you had the hots for each other. Everyone could see that."

"They could not."

"Don't fool yourself," Ian said drily. "Of course they could. But you kept your hands to yourself. I didn't think you could do it, but you did. So why now, twelve years later? Why couldn't you keep your pants on?"

All Evan could do was shake his head. "I can't tell you."

"Can't or won't?"

Evan straightened and pulled his hands out of his pockets. The knowledge that he had been so transparent grated.

Irritation was beginning to rise. He looked Ian directly in the eye, refusing to back down.

"*Won't.* Anna may be your sister, but she's a woman, too. I'm not going to tell you why I'm—" He stopped and corrected himself. "Why I *was* attracted to her. All I can say is that I wasn't in that bed alone."

Ian spun away with an oath. "Don't go there, man."

"Then don't ask me to," Evan said harshly. "Shit, Ian. I'm groping in the dark here. I want to do the right thing, but God help me if I know what that is."

"And all Anna wants is to get married?"

Evan shrugged. "She asked if I *would* marry her. She didn't say if that's what she *wanted.*"

"But you said no."

"We'd both be miserable." Evan paused. For a moment, he found himself back in the coffee shop, looking at a vacant chair and a half-empty mug of tea. He shook his head firmly. "It's the wrong reason to get married."

"Yeah. You're probably right," Ian conceded. He sighed, went back to his seat and swallowed more wine. He was silent for a long time, his eyes on the far wall. Evan walked back to the sofa and sat. He picked up his glass, took a deep drink, then put it back down. He didn't know what else there was to say, so he said nothing.

"When are you going to tell Ma and Pop?"

Evan winced. "Soon. I have to talk to Anna first."

"So that's why you're going with Pop?"

"Partly," Evan said with a snort of laughter. "Partly to keep him from going off half-cocked. I tried to stop him, but he'd already bought tickets."

"He's pretty determined to fix things for her." Ian looked over at Evan. "He's going to be pissed when he finds out about you and Anna, you know. Delay's just going to make him madder."

Evan nodded. Truer words had never been spoken. He leaned forward and picked up his glass again, but didn't drink. The spilled wine had almost dried and left a ring on the wood, darkening it. He absently traced the circle of wet with one finger.

"How'd you figure it out?" He glanced at Ian briefly, then back down. "About Anna and me."

"I didn't actually know for sure until tonight. I suspected something was going on between you two that day we all met."

"What? How?"

"You didn't tease her even once, McKenzie. You *always* tease Anna and it stuck out when you didn't." Ian shrugged. "Then Pop said she was pregnant and I did the math, but I wasn't sure. It seemed too crazy to be true."

"I'll say. I still can't believe it."

"Look, you want some advice?"

"Not especially."

Ian cleared his throat. "The way I see it, you guys have been headed here for a long time. Since she was in high school."

"Trust me, I haven't been headed *here*," Evan said decisively. "No way was a baby in my plans."

"You know what I mean. Why not see where it takes you?"

Evan laughed. "This is not a road either of us wants to take. It was just a…" He hesitated, not wanting to piss Ian off again. "A detour that I think we both regret."

"Do you? Really?"

Evan didn't hesitate. "Definitely."

Ian drained the last of his wine and stood up. "Well. I've got to go."

"That's it? You're not going to beat my brains in?"

"Not tonight," Ian said with a chuckle. "Maybe after Anna gets done with you."

Evan stood, following him down the short hall to the front door. Ian grabbed his coat and put it on. When he turned back to Evan, his face was serious. "You need to take care of this Evan. A kid needs a father. And that's not just because she's my sister, but because it's the right thing to do."

"I'd already figured that out," Evan agreed irritably.

"Hey, man, don't get so defensive," Ian said as he pulled the door open. He paused in the doorway, then turned back. "You might want to review how you got here, though. Not the pregnancy part, but why after all this time, you and Anna took that 'detour' together."

"I told you, it was just a…an impulse."

"Were you both drunk?"

"No."

"Okay. And you both could pass for intelligent adults. So what tipped you over the edge?"

Ian's dark eyes seemed to bore into his brain; they were too much like Anna's for comfort at this moment. Evan didn't flinch under the stern regard, but remained silent. He just lost control, that's all it was.

"Love's a funny thing," Ian said, a slight smile turning up one corner of his mouth. "When you least expect, it sneaks up on you."

"I told you, I *don't* love Anna. I don't love any woman."

"Well, I guess you should know." With that, Ian stepped outside and closed the door.

As he stared at the space where his friend had stood, a shiver ran over Evan's skin. It was just the cold, damp night air, he told himself. Ian had no idea what was going on between him and Anna. He was married and happy and applied that bandage to heal all the world's problems.

Going back into the living room, Evan picked up his glass and swallowed the last of the wine in it. He put the glasses and bottle in the kitchen, then cleaned up the spill on the coffee table. Turning off the lights, he went upstairs to his bedroom. He was tired and decided to turn in early; tomorrow would be a long day.

Lying in the darkness, Evan rehashed his whole encounter with Ian. It hadn't been as bad as he had feared. Ian had been angry, but he hadn't slugged him or even terminated their friendship. But, then, Ian wasn't Patrick. And certainly not Antonio. Sighing, Evan closed his eyes, forcing himself to sleep. Tomorrow he would face Anna again. Maybe they could come up with a common solution for their mutual problems. One that didn't entail losing the best family he had.

Chapter Nine

"All right. I'll make the changes and have revised plans to you by next week. Thanks. Bye."

Anna cradled the phone receiver and made a few more notes on her set of drawings. She glanced up as Carl walked into her office, motioning with one hand to silence him before he could speak. When she had finished writing down her thought, she looked up with a smile.

"Sorry. If I stop in the middle, I lose it."

"A great idea might be lost forever." He came to stand beside her at the drafting table. "Artie said to tell you to check your in-box. He sent the specs for Creekmore to you a few minutes ago."

"Oh, good. He was quick. I'll pass them on to Engstrom so they can get their numbers together."

"How're things going?"

Anna leaned an elbow on the table, twirling a pen between her fingers. "Arcata has slowed since the client's at a wedding this week in Palm Beach. I have a meeting up there next Tuesday to go over preliminaries. The Clairemont is out to bid and Houston is bickering with the contractor on the final punch list."

"Problem?"

"Only if those crazy Texans reach for their rifles," Anna

said with a grin. "I'm mediating and they're working it out. We'll get it settled."

"And my favorite architect?" Carl's eyes were kind, his tone concerned. "How's she doing?"

"Your favorite architect is Ken Allsop," Anna said, shaking the pen at him. "But that's probably because you sleep with him."

"Okay, how's my *second* favorite architect?" Carl admitted with a laugh.

Anna shrugged. "She's fine."

"Morning sickness?"

"That's doing just fine, too, thank you very much."

Carl winced. "Bad, huh?"

"I get up, I throw up and I eat dry toast. It's usually gone by midmorning." Anna laughed at herself. "I have yet to lose it on a client, so I think I'm beating the odds."

"Great, so I'm the only one who's experienced the pleasure."

"You hated that tie anyway. I never knew why you wore it."

"It was a gift." Carl's eyes danced with humor. "From Ken's mother."

Anna stared at him for a moment, then let out a peal of laughter. "You should thank me, then. I did you a favor."

"Um, no," Carl said, shaking his head. "That was *not* a favor."

They both laughed.

Anna remembered how horrified she had been when she had lost it all over her boss the day she returned from Crab Creek. After cleaning up—and her profuse apologies—Carl had coaxed the truth out of her. Anna had magnified her embarrassment by crying all over him. Carl had patted her back and offered tissues. When she was calm again, he had offered to help in any way he could.

In some strange way, the incident had made them closer friends than before. It was a balm to have such unquestioning support. Unsurprisingly, she hadn't heard a peep out of Evan. Her father called every day, though, always circling around to the same question that she refused to answer. The recollection of those irritating, insistent conversations— and the silence from Evan—made her appreciate the man standing with her now.

Impulsively, Anna reached out and hugged Carl. He returned the embrace, then stood back, his hands at her waist. "Thanks, but what was that for?"

"For being such a good man." Anna smiled up at him. "You are a rare breed."

Carl chuckled and opened his mouth to speak. Before a sound came out, there was a shout from the door of Anna's office.

"I knew I would catch him!"

Anna's head whipped around and she saw her father standing in the doorway. His expression was thunderous as he pointed an accusatory finger at her.

"Pop! What are you—"

"You will not get away with this," Antonio said in a roar. As he started across the room, Anna was shocked to see Evan walk in behind him.

"Oh, my God," she whispered, ignoring her father to drink in the sight of Evan. Weak-kneed, she clung to Carl's arms for a second, her head in a whirl of helpless hope. Had Evan changed his mind? Did he want to start over? Ask her to marry him? Why else would he have flown across the country?

Her momentary fantasy allowed Antonio to pick up steam. "I will have satisfaction for what you have done to my daughter."

Jerked back to reality, Anna glanced up at Carl who

stood openmouthed, staring at Antonio. He was as surprised as she, yet for obviously completely different reasons. Her father was charging at him like a madman. Anna swiftly interposed herself between the two men.

"Wait a minute, Pop. It's not what you—"

Antonio stopped just short of them and shook his fist at Carl. "Hide behind a woman, will you? Coward! I will not stand for it. I will not!"

"Stop it!" Putting her hands out, she pushed against her father's chest as he stepped closer, reaching around her to grab for his prey.

"Jeez, Anna," Carl said from behind her. "This is your father? I bet I know where you get your temper."

"Who are you?" Antonio ignored Anna and lunged for Carl again. "Identify yourself!"

"Evan, *do* something," she said over Antonio's shoulder.

Evan's face was set, his eyes like polished emeralds as he glared at Carl. "Better answer the question, buddy."

"Have you both gone crazy? Carl's my *boss*."

"That explains it," Evan said, stepping closer, his fists clenched. "He's the guy you said you *weren't* dating."

"So you take advantage of the women who work for you." Antonio scowled at Carl. "This is disgraceful."

There was a burst of laughter from over Anna's shoulder as Carl said, "I got Anna pregnant. *That's* a good one."

"So you admit it!"

"He does not!" Anna said desperately, looking up into her father's face. Antonio pressed forward, forcing her back into Carl. "We work together—"

"It didn't look like work to me." Evan eyes narrowed as he glowered at the man behind her.

"What can I say? Anna's more than *just* another employee," Carl said with a laugh.

"You laugh at me? At my daughter?" Antonio had stilled and his face flushed a deep red. A stream of Italian came from him that Anna couldn't translate. She understood that he was furious, though.

"Calm down, Pop," Anna said. "Carl, tell him you weren't laughing."

"But I *was* laughing," Carl said. "This is better than *Springer*."

"You will pay for such disrespect!"

"Carl, *please*. He's seriously pissed," Anna said.

"No. Go ahead, Carl. Keep it up," Evan said. "I want to watch him pound you into a bloody pulp. Then I'll take a turn at you."

"This matter must be settled between men," Antonio said, picking Anna up as if she weighed nothing. He handed her to Evan, who grasped her waist and drew her against his lean hard body.

For a second, just a second, despite the craziness, Anna melted. The close embrace reminded her of too much and made her ache for more. Then she looked up and her gaze collided with Evan's. The glittering green stare was full of scorn that brought her back to her senses.

"Let go of me, you idiot," she ordered.

"Forget it," he said grimly. "I don't want you getting hurt when your dad teaches loverboy a lesson."

As Anna fought to get free, Antonio was rolling up his sleeves, each fold of his cuffs determined, deliberate.

Carl was watching the older man, amusement clear on his face. "Wait a minute. Before we get too far along, maybe we should get a paternity test. Just to be sure."

"Carl, please!"

Her boss ignored Anna's plea. Her father was still cursing in Italian. Evan's hold was tight; much as she wriggled, he would not release her. Disaster was about to strike and there was nothing she could do to stop this farce.

"Pop, listen to me!" Anna's voice rose to a shriek. "He can't be the father. He's *gay!*"

Antonio stopped his folding, obviously stunned by this revelation.

"I *could* be the father." Carl turned to Anna. Despite his stern expression, she could see amusement twinkling in his eyes. "Just because I'm gay *doesn't* mean I'm sterile!"

Anna felt her skin heat and knew a blush was turning her bright red. When she pulled away from Evan this time, he let her go.

"You're dating a gay guy?" Evan asked, looking bewildered.

Anna ignored his ridiculous question and glared at her father. "Pop, you owe my boss an apology."

Antonio looked hard at the other man, then said, "A father must protect his daughter, especially his youngest one." He stood straight and tall and didn't look sorry in the least.

Anna put a hand to her forehead where an ache was beginning to spread. "That is not an apology," she said through gritted teeth.

"For what do I apologize?" Antonio asked haughtily. "I did not hit this man."

"For acting like a complete nut, would be a place to start," Anna said, throwing her hands up in frustration. "For embarrassing me and insulting Carl."

"How did I do these things?" Antonio scoffed. He turned to Carl, grabbed the other man's arms and gave him a little shake while eyeing him closely. "Did I insult you?"

Obviously bemused, Carl shook his head. "Not in the least, Mr. Berzani. If anyone insulted me, it was Anna."

Antonio clapped him once on the shoulders and turned to his daughter. "You see, he is fine. No harm done."

Anna felt like screaming in aggravation or laughing in hysteria, she wasn't sure which. "Could you excuse us, Carl?" she asked, keeping her voice level. "I need to talk to these two cavemen. Alone."

"Are you sure?" Carl asked, touching her arm lightly.

"Don't worry about me. They're the ones in danger."

With a glance at the other two men, Carl walked to the door. There, he turned and looked back at Antonio. "Mr. Berzani, if Anna needs a father for her child, I'll be the first in line."

"That is very generous of you," Antonio said gravely.

"Anna's a dear friend," Carl said, his tone just as serious. "I want you to know that she has people here who love her. The *real* father, whoever he is, is missing out on something special."

As Carl spoke, Anna saw Evan stiffen. Instead of speaking, he went to the windows and stood looking out, hands in his pockets. It was as if what had transpired didn't concern him at all. His indifference further fired her anger.

Carl closed the door behind him and her father let out a huff of breath. "He is a kind man, that is clear. I am pleased."

Anna turned to her father. "Is that *all* you have to say for yourself, Pop?"

"I want what is best for you, Anna Maria," he said, coming to her and putting his hands on her shoulders. "Even your good friend sees that you need a husband."

"He said if I wanted a *father,* not that I needed a husband," Anna said sharply.

Antonio ignored this clarification. "The father *must* take his share in this situation. You cannot raise a child alone."

"How is forcing the guy to marry me going to accomplish anything? What makes you think he'll stick around, anyway? You can force him to the altar at gunpoint, I guess, but as soon as you're gone, he's gone. Then I'm right back where I started from."

"You do not know how hard it will be."

"I know that it's plenty hard *now*."

"See! And this is only the beginning," Antonio said, completely missing her point. He slid his hands to hers and gripped them firmly. The dark eyes she had inherited locked with hers, his expression solemn. "When you were a baby, I stayed up many late nights with you so your mother could sleep. I changed your diapers. I read to you at bedtime. I loved you. I cared for you. So many things that a father does for a child. A mother cannot do it all by herself."

Anna spun away from her father's hold. She caught sight of Evan, who had turned back toward them. His face was unreadable and Anna felt an ache in her heart. "But the father of my child doesn't love me, Pop."

"He will learn to love you. Besides, it is his duty."

"Duty's no substitute for love." Tears sprang into her throat and she had to swallow before speaking again. "Isn't that right, Evan?"

The question seemed to shock him. He jerked to attention, then slid his hands out of his pockets so his arms hung down at his sides. "No. It isn't."

The answer was no more or less than she had expected, but her temper flared again. He stood there, offering nothing. Had he come all this way to tell her that?

"How could you do this, Evan?" she asked. The tears had welled up in her eyes. "You sat on that airplane for seven hours and said *nothing* to him?"

"Evan is not to blame for this," Antonio said. "He did not want to make this trip."

Anna ignored her father and waited for Evan's defense, for him to speak the truth, but nothing came.

"Are you that ashamed of me?" Her voice wobbled and she felt sick.

"Of course not."

There was no hesitation in Evan's reply, but Anna didn't believe his answer. If not shame, why else had Evan worked so hard to hide the fact that he was the father of her child? Why else had he not told her parents? Why else had he not called her?

"No one is ashamed, Anna." Antonio stood next to Evan. "He came to defend your honor."

Evan remained silent. His face was still, his green gaze stoic.

"I'm sorry I've been such a disappointment to you. Getting pregnant was not my plan." Anna looked at the two men and felt the heat of her anger cycle down to a cold sorrow. "But you know what? I've started to look forward to it. But you wouldn't know that, would you? Neither of you. No one has bothered to ask what I think about this, if I'm happy or sad or scared or angry."

Anna crossed her arms over her chest in an attempt to give comfort where none was being offered. "From the moment I found out that I was pregnant, there hasn't been one *second* of concern for what I think and feel. All you want to do is pin the blame on some mystery man. You want to *solve my problem*. Well, guess what? A child isn't a problem, it's a life, an opportunity, a *joy*." Her voice rose and she stopped, taking a deep breath to steady herself. "I have had enough of being your personal crisis."

"Anna—"

"No more." Anna held up a hand, interrupting her father

before he could finish. "I want you to leave. Now. I have a job to do and you've disrupted my day long enough."

Antonio opened his mouth to speak again, but Evan took him by the arm. "She's right, Pop. Let's get out of here."

Anna watched as Evan herded Antonio in front of him and out of the office. At the door, he turned back to her. "I'm sorry, Anna. Really. I'll...call you later."

"You've had a month to talk to me," Anna said, her heart cold. "At this point, I have no interest in anything you have to say."

He seemed about to speak again, then obviously thought better of it. Stepping through the door, he closed it softly behind himself. The click of the latch felt very final.

Knees weak, Anna fumbled for the chair in front of her desk. Sitting, she put her face in her hands, pressing her fingertips lightly against her eyelids. Her eyes burned, but they were dry now. She had no tears for anyone, not herself or Evan or the baby. It wouldn't last, though. She knew there were many tears in her future. Too many to count.

EVAN SIPPED HIS SODA, fingers toying with the end of his seat belt. Next to him, Antonio snored softly, head tilted against the window. How he could sleep, Evan didn't know. Maybe Antonio didn't feel he had done anything wrong. Maybe he hadn't. Maybe just defending your child, even when you're wrong, absolved you. Evan wished he felt the same—that he *could* feel the same. He had screwed up and he knew it.

With a sigh, he leaned his head back and stared absently at the overhead storage bins that lined the aisle. He didn't know what San Francisco's official motto was, but for him it might as well be City of Disasters. On his first visit, he acted in a way unrecognizable to himself. This trip, the same was true—though the memories he carried back were painful rather than pleasurable.

So many unanswerable questions swirled around in his head. Why had he let Antonio cause such a scene? Why had the sight of Anna in her boss's arms infuriated him? He didn't love her, so why should it matter if there was some other man in her life? Why hadn't he answered Anna's question and defended himself?

Closing his eyes, Evan tried to imagine the entire scene playing out differently. He would have restrained Antonio immediately, calmed him or hustled him out of the office before he could continue his rant. Then he would ask Anna if she would talk to him, just the two of them.

Calmly, clearly, he would tell her how he could support her and the baby, expanding what he had told her that day in the coffee shop. He would tell her how he planned to be a father, how he *could* do it from a distance. After she saw how sincere he was, how much sense he made, after they had agreed to a plan, then he would go to her family and tell them the truth. They would understand that he meant to do his duty. His road to atonement could finally begin.

Opening his eyes, Evan looked over at Antonio. The older man snorted and shifted, but remained asleep. Evan imagined the moment when he would break the news to Antonio. A humorless smile twisted Evan's lips. If he told him now, Antonio would go into a rage, far worse than the one he had unleashed in Anna's office. An air marshal was likely to pull a gun on both of them. At best, they would end up in jail and be banned from flying for the rest of their natural lives.

Finishing his drink, Evan set the glass aside. His head was already aching from drinking too much wine the night before at the restaurant that Antonio's cousin owned. It had been a typical Berzani affair: tons of food, gallons of wine, loud arguments and people of all ages. Every relative in the city, no matter how distant or dubious, had attended.

Evan had been thankful for the chaos. It had kept him from brooding too much. Anna had refused to answer her phone and, when he went to her condo, she was either gone or not opening the door. He had retreated, disheartened, but determined to succeed in settling things between them. When he got back home, after she had had time to cool down, he would try again.

With a sigh, Evan tilted the seat back and tried to sleep or at least relax. It had been less than two weeks since the news of the pregnancy. No wonder he felt confused and befuddled. No wonder this trip to San Francisco was such a disaster. He had to give himself time. And give Anna time, too. Things would get better. They had to.

Chapter Ten

"We will sit in front," Antonio announced as he, Elaine and Anna walked down the main corridor of city hall. "I do not care what Evan says. I know politics. If the commissioners must look us in the eye, they will certainly grant us permission."

"Fine by me," Anna said. At least they could agree on *something,* she thought wryly.

Which made for a nice change. Her father may have retreated from the battlefield in San Francisco, but the war had continued for the five weeks since then. The salvos were lobbed via e-mail from one coast to the other, with endless rounds of arguments fired over the phone on the same topic. Her father was determined to solve her "problem." Anna was just as determined to prove him wrong. She could manage without a man. Especially a reluctant one.

Her conversations with Evan held a disheartening symmetry to those she had with her father. He would call and offer a deal—shared custody, joint parenting, child support or some combination of all—and she would refuse. The only commitment he would agree to was fatherhood, a fact he couldn't deny anyway. Her aching heart wished he would propose marriage, or at least living together, but Evan never broached the subject. Anna knew she shouldn't be surprised. His anticommitment streak ran deep. Still, it hurt to be rejected.

That feeling of rejection was intensified by his inability to admit the truth publicly. When she asked if he had told her parents yet, Evan hedged, he needed more time, he needed a plan before he broached the news. Every excuse sounded like more evidence that he was ashamed of her and his child. The idea, first spawned that awful day of revelation at her parents' house, ate at her. She might understand his fear of marriage and commitment, but his shame was the one thing she could not forgive.

When Evan asked about the baby and her health, she answered tersely. What was the point of details when they weren't going to be raising this child together? The whole thing was painful, sad and demoralizing, so much so that she had no intention of even seeing Evan on this trip. She just couldn't stand the misery.

Near a pair of wide-open double doors, a cardboard placard on an easel announced Planning Commission, 6:30 p.m. Following her parents inside, Anna looked around. It seemed much like every other city meeting room she had been in over the years. There were neat rows of chairs, an aisle down the middle, a podium off to the left. A long table with a navy blue skirt and microphones on it stretched across the front. Flags of the United States and Maryland flanked a clock on the wall behind. She had to smile a little. The size of these rooms changed, but the immutable ambiance of bureaucracy remained the same.

Antonio and Elaine led the way to seats facing the main table. Seating herself next to her father, Anna smoothed her skirt under her. The zipper at her waistband, hidden by her suit jacket, slipped down a couple of notches. Surreptitiously, she reached back and slid it into place and squirmed in her chair. The small safety pin, no match for her expanding waistline, must have popped off.

"You need a pillow?" he asked. "I have one in the car."

"No, Pop. I'm fine."

"Do you have everything for your speech?"

It was the eighty-seventh time he had asked that particular question—or at least it seemed like it. Holding on to her patience with both hands, Anna opened her briefcase and pulled out a thick manila file folder, then set the case under her chair. She flipped through her notes to show her father they were in order. She also had a copy of the paperwork each of the commissioners had been sent: scale drawings of the building, elevations and perspectives showing the finished site, complete with happy pedestrians walking around.

"See? It's all here, Pop," she assured him.

"Good." He nodded once, then turned to face the front, his arms crossed over his chest.

Other people began to fill the chairs around them. A tall man stepped behind the table and fiddled with a microphone. Bending over he said, "Good evening, everyone. If you'll all take a seat, we'll get tonight's meeting started."

There was a general shuffle and scrape of chairs. Four other people joined the man behind the table: three men and a woman. Anna perused the faces of the five commissioners. They would make or break her project. Someone slipped into the seat next to her, jostling her elbow. Glancing over, the polite smile on her face shattered like glass when she saw Evan McKenzie.

"What are you doing here?" she whispered angrily.

"Pop called and—"

"I don't care what he said!" Her voice was nearly a growl. "I told you not to show up tonight."

Antonio reached across her and the two men shook hands. Anna was furious. She had specifically told Evan to stay away; this meeting would be stressful enough without his presence. Before she could tell Evan to get lost, the chairman rustled through his papers and cleared his throat.

"Thank you for joining us tonight. We have a full agenda, so we're going to have to move right along to get through it all before eight-thirty. First, I'll call attendance for the meeting."

Anna lost the rest of his words, too unsettled by Evan. Their chairs were set close together. One broad shoulder pressed against hers, his long legs just inches away. The crisp scent of his cologne enveloped her senses. It aggravated her, reminded her of a night she did not want to remember. She cursed her father and Evan both: one for demanding attendance and the other for dutifully obeying the summons.

Everyone rose for the Pledge of Allegiance. The minutes of the previous meeting were approved and the chairman got down to business. "The first item on the agenda is the proposed liquor license change for Crabby Cal's at Seventh and Main. Is Cal Sandler here tonight?"

A portly man in a baggy brown suit went to the podium. Anna listened with half an ear as the commissioners asked a few routine questions. She slid a glance at Evan, but his eyes were fixed on the proceedings. Against her will, her gaze traveled along the clean line of his profile, pausing on the thick blond lashes screening those incredible green eyes. His hair was brushed neatly, just touching the collar of his white shirt. A pale yellow tie was knotted at his throat.

Suddenly, Anna remembered tugging at a similar tie—this one green—then his hands pushing hers aside to dispense with the impediment to passion. A wash of heat sped through her veins that had nothing to do with anger. The memory made her even more irritated with Evan—and with herself. Why did he have to be here?

She stiffened when Evan looked over at her, catching her staring. One of his eyebrows rose and there was a question in his eyes. For a moment, Anna forgot where she was. Her tongue came out to moisten dry lips. His gaze dropped to her mouth. It was as though time had stopped and they were alone in some faraway place.

"Yes! She is here." Her father said loudly, poking her sharply in the side. "Anna Maria, they are calling you."

Anna jerked to attention and got to her feet. A blush heated her face and she swore a silent litany at Evan as she went to the podium, though she knew her own weakness had tripped her up. "Mr. Chairman, Commissioners. My name is Anna Berzani."

Taking a steadying breath, Anna launched into a brief description of the project. By the third sentence she was calm again, focused on her presentation. Her voice was firm and clear as she made her case. She met the eyes of each of the commissioners, speaking to them directly. They wore various expressions of interest, boredom and, strangely, in the case of the lone woman on the panel, a scowl of irritation.

"The project will foster neighboring business and add a number of benefits to our community. And so I ask for your approval on this plan," Anna concluded. "Thank you for your time."

"Thank you, Ms. Berzani." The chairman adjusted his microphone and turned to his colleagues. "Questions?"

"I have several," the scowling woman said, leaning forward into her microphone.

Anna thought she saw the chairman roll his eyes. "All right, Ms. Shermer, you have the floor."

"First, I have a copy of my concerns for each commissioner." The woman passed a stack of stapled papers down the table. The other commissioners, caught off guard, flipped through them with a rustle that echoed through the sound system. Then, eyes narrowed, the woman stared at Anna for a second.

"Ms. Berzani, this property is zoned for marine and light manufacturing, and you have applied for a variance to change it to multiuse residential, retail and marine."

"Yes, ma'am," Anna agreed, uncertain where the question was leading.

The woman smiled but there was no warmth in it. "Do you realize that this project is going to remove one of the last working boatyards in our city? If we approve your plans, a piece of our history is going to disappear, too."

Antonio snorted loudly. Anna glanced over and saw her parents exchanging an amused look. Evan did not look equally entertained: he was scowling.

"The boatyard is not that old, Ms. Shermer. When my clients bought the property nearly thirty years ago, it was a derelict fish-canning plant, with equally dilapidated docks," Anna explained. "I know we are proposing a large change, but my par—er, *clients,* believe it is in keeping with the trends and progress of the community. The area has become more and more gentrified, with the commensurate desire for services to provide for that new population. Plus, there is a demand for waterfront access that the yard doesn't provide. Our project will answer both those needs."

"What about those people who lose their jobs when the yard closes?"

From the corner of her eye, Anna caught sight of her father leaning over and whispering to Evan. He was not so amused now. "Any losses at the boatyard will be more than replaced by the new retail and restaurant."

"But at severely reduced wages, no doubt." The woman pursed her lips. "Busboys don't make the same as skilled boat builders."

"Hah!" Antonio exclaimed. "But *we* don't get tips."

The chairman rapped his gavel.

"We don't build boats, anyway. We fix them," Antonio announced. Elaine patted his arm and shushed him.

"Silence, please!" the chairman demanded. "Continue, Ms. Berzani."

"This is a family business and the employees are part of that family. My clients will ensure that all of them find jobs at other yards on the Chesapeake," Anna said mildly. Inside she was starting to steam. "So we are actually *adding* jobs."

"Indeed." Ms. Shermer slipped on a pair of half glasses and looked down at the paper in front of her. "Moving on. Ms. Berzani, how is your project going to affect the traffic patterns through this neighborhood?"

"Bayshore is currently a commercial street and we don't anticipate adding more traffic than the yard already has. The new residences should actually decrease congestion during the day."

"I find that hard to believe! A restaurant and several retail shops reducing congestion? As I recall—" she shuffled through some of the papers "—yes, Bayshore is the only arterial serving that area."

"We did a preliminary traffic study and—"

"I saw it. But you can only *extrapolate* from that," Commissioner Shermer said, looking at her over the tops of her half-glasses. "The fact is, you won't actually know how much impact it has until after the damage is done."

Anna held on to her temper. Where was this attack

coming from? That it was an attack, she had no doubt. Replacing an old boatyard and worn-out sheds with a well-designed building benefited nearly everyone in town. Besides, others had built much larger developments along this strip of water over the past five years with the commission's blessing. A simple project like this did not warrant this intense grilling.

Anna looked over at Evan. His grim expression didn't help. The fact that he had a tight grip on her father's arm didn't bode well, either. Antonio's narrow-eyed glower told her he was nearing explosion level. She rushed to the counterattack, hoping to forestall a scene.

"The study showed that the road can handle an increase of two hundred cars with no improvements," Anna said evenly. "The data on page thirteen clearly shows this."

"And what about the noise?" Ms. Shermer asked, her tone cold. "That restaurant will be open *far* later than a boatyard. And serving alcohol, no doubt. Families live in that neighborhood, Ms. Berzani."

"Who is this woman?" Antonio demanded. Evan pulled him back as the chairman used his gavel again and leveled a stern stare at the older man. Though he lowered his voice, Antonio's whisper carried clearly. "*She* is the one making trouble. Not me!"

Anna felt a throb of pain begin at one temple. Trying to ignore it—and her father—she continued, "We've discussed this with the liquor control board. No hard liquor will be served on-site, only beer and wine. And I can name several other full-service bars along the waterfront that thrive without late-night partying."

"Beer and boats have *never* been a good combination." The woman shook her head and took off her glasses, tossing them on the table in front of her in a gesture of irritated disdain. "I don't like this project one little bit, Ms. Berzani.

There are too many unexplored repercussions that could spell disaster. And our waterfront has become *too* gentrified with too little thought about what it is doing to our maritime community. We simply cannot discard the past in blind pursuit of the future." ̄

Her father growled something Anna couldn't quite make out. She resolutely kept her eyes on the board members, hoping Evan would control Antonio.

"I understand your concerns, Ms. Shermer," Anna said, lying through her teeth. "However, we have studied the effects thoroughly—"

"Really? I don't see that exhibited here at all." She waved a hand at the documents in front of her.

Anna took a breath, anger rising in her throat. "We have applied for funding with the Small Community Development Fund. As I'm sure you are aware, this stage of the permits must be completed in ten days to qualify. We—"

"Ah, so that explains your rush and this shoddy research," Ms. Shermer said with a smirk. "You may have a deadline, Ms. Berzani, but I see no reason to disrupt the lives of several thousand people because of you and your clients' greed." The woman turned to the others sitting to either side of her. "What does the rest of the board think about all this? Mr. Chairman?"

He cleared his throat. "Well, Miriam, you certainly raise some serious questions. Apparently I haven't taken as close a look at this as I ought to have."

There was a general murmur of agreement from the other commissioners. Anna stared at Ms. Shermer and felt her temper begin to boil over. Why was the woman trying to crush the project?

"This is crazy!" Anna began. "I have provided all the doc—"

Before she could say more, Evan suddenly gripped

her arm and pulled her back from the podium and the microphone.

"Mr. Chairman, Commissioners, if I might beg your indulgence," he said, raising the microphone to suit his height. "My name is Evan McKenzie and I am one of the applicants for this proposal. Unfortunately, we are short of time. Our goal is to bring more people and more business to the waterfront community. We need SCDF funding to do it. Is it possible to have the time to answer Ms. Shermer's concerns and still make our deadline?"

"Why should we accommodate—"

"Please, sirs and ma'am," Evan said overtop of Ms. Shermer. "Let us prove to you that the benefits of this project *far* outweigh the deficits. If you grant us another hearing in one week, I'm sure we can allay your concerns."

"That would mean a special session," the chairman said slowly.

"That is an unnecessary burden on this commission," Ms. Shermer snapped.

Another commissioner, an older gentleman who seemed to have doodled on a yellow pad throughout the discussion, suddenly spoke up. "I think this is a jim-dandy project. I talked to a few folks this week who would like that yard gone and something prettier in its place. I think we should honor the request." He nodded at Anna and Evan.

"What the heck. I'll do it," said a second man and a third shrugged his shoulders and agreed, as well.

"Well, Ms. Shermer?" the chairman asked.

With ill-concealed annoyance at being outvoted, she scowled. "Fine."

The chairman turned back to Anna and Evan. "One week, then. A special hearing at the same time, in this room. Until then, the matter is tabled. Ms. Shermer, do you have an extra copy of your objections for Mr. McKenzie and Ms. Berzani?"

The older woman shoved one of the documents to the edge of the table in front of her. Anna walked over to pick it up, meeting Commissioner Shermer's eyes for a moment and sharing mutual, silent hostility.

"Thank you all," Evan said, then stepped away from the podium.

They resumed their seats and the next applicant came forward. Anna's father grabbed her fingers in a bone-crushing squeeze. His dark eyes were still full of fire, but he gave her an approving nod before reaching for Evan's hand and giving it the same treatment. Elaine leaned over, her eyes worried. Anna tried to smile reassuringly.

Anna thumbed through Commissioner Shermer's objections. They were mostly a detailed list of Grade A manure. But given only one week, they would be difficult to counter with solid evidence, reason and data. Evan reached over and took the document from her hands. His eyes narrowed as he read. After he had skimmed it, his gaze met hers. Anna shook her head, admitting that their project was doomed. Her hands clenched, fingers knotting together. Evan looked as discouraged as she felt. What would her parents do now?

To her surprise, Evan reached out and put his hand over hers. His clasp was warm, offering solace—solace she wanted to take. Slowly, Anna relaxed and he insinuated his fingers around hers. Her anger toward him had faded. Instead, fury burned inside for Commissioner Shermer.

The meeting continued while Anna's attention wandered elsewhere. She had fought two battles tonight and lost both: Evan had regained a hold on her heart and Ms.

Shermer had shot down her plans for her parents' future. At the moment, she could not decide which loss had done the most damage.

THE MEETING DRONED ON through the next presentation. Those that followed Anna seemed to have better luck securing approval, but Evan hardly heard a word. He was still focused on their own loss. He knew exactly why Miriam Shermer had attacked Anna. It had nothing to do with Anna, the Berzanis or the waterfront community. It had everything to do with him and Miriam's niece, his former girlfriend, Kippy Shermer. This was revenge, pure and simple.

Kippy hadn't wanted to break up, but she had been pleasant enough about it. He knew she had expected to lure him back. After his night with Anna—and the aftermath—Evan had been completely uninterested. Kippy had obviously decided to make sure he knew she didn't like that. Anna was going to be furious when he told her. How he could fix the damage, Evan had no idea.

Anna shifted slightly, her fingers sliding against his. Evan knew he should pull away, but he didn't. He had impulsively linked them together to give comfort and now he was fighting the desire for something more. Sitting next to her had been torture, especially when he could feel her eyes on his skin. He wanted so much more than just her gaze to touch him.

Her thumb brushed his and she leaned close to whisper in his ear. The warm wash of her breath sent a shiver through him. "Let's get out of here before the next presentation."

Evan nodded, releasing her hand reluctantly. She turned to her father and he saw Antonio nod. Anna collected her briefcase. As soon as the commissioners cast their vote in favor of the petitioner, Anna rose to her feet. Evan followed suit, catching the victorious smirk on Miriam Shermer's face. Before he turned up the aisle, he gave her a deliberate smile and wink. The brief flare of outrage on her face was worth whatever it had cost. They slipped out the door and Evan closed it carefully behind them.

Antonio charged down the hall several paces, before turning. "That woman is a *viper.*" He shook his finger at them. "There is no other word for her."

"Now, Tonio, we mustn't—"

"You told me she was on our side!" Antonio said, his dark eyes boring twin holes into Evan. "You said this would be a big piece of cake."

Evan shook his head. "She told me last month that we had her support."

"Bah! So much for your connections," the older man said, waving a hand.

"*She* was the one you talked about in my office?" Anna asked Evan.

"It doesn't matter. We must use *my* connections," Antonio interrupted, pacing up the hallway and back. "I have just had a thought. Jimmy Johnson is a city council member and my best customer. I will go to him right now and he will straighten this out."

"It's eight o'clock, Pop. I don't think—"

"Take Anna home," Antonio directed Evan and clapped a hand on his shoulder. "Do not blame yourself. Sometimes these things happen in politics. I will take care of it from here."

With that, he strode off. Elaine sighed, gave Anna and Evan a the-things-I-put-up-with look and trotted after him.

Evan and Anna watched them go, then she turned to face him. Her eyes were cool, her gaze speculative. "That woman was on a mission to kill this project, Evan. What did you do to her?"

Evan knew there was no point in delaying the inevitable. If he had learned one thing lately, it was that the longer you waited to tell the truth, the worse the consequences became. And he couldn't afford to pile more deception onto the one he was already hiding from the Berzanis.

Bracing himself, he looked her straight in the eyes. "She's Kippy's aunt."

"Kippy?" Anna blinked at him in confusion. "The blonde with big—"

Evan winced. "Yeah, her."

"But you said you broke up with her."

"I did. She just didn't think I meant it." He ran a hand through his hair. "I didn't think she'd be so vindictive."

"Oh, for pity's sake, Evan." Anna put one hand on her hip as she glared at him. "I could have told you that and I spent about sixty seconds with the woman."

"Okay, fine, I'm an idiot," Evan said, trying to keep his voice down. "I admit it. I should have dumped her *after* we got approval."

"So, you screwed Kippy and now *we're* screwed," Anna said bitterly.

"You want me to go apologize and ask her out again?" he asked harshly. "Say the word and—"

"Stop it!" She put up a hand as if to ward off his words. "Please tell me you at least broke up with her in person."

"What, you think I texted her?" Evan's temper flared hotter.

"When you dumped me, I got no communication at all. A text message would have made my day."

The words hit Evan like a slap. Sucking in a deep breath, he held it, then let it out slowly. "I called you."

"Yeah," she said flatly. "After you found out I was

pregnant. When you couldn't pretend we hadn't slept together."

He looked away, then back, meeting her gaze squarely. They had wandered off course. He wanted to blame her for that, but Anna wasn't at fault here; he was. "I broke things off politely with Kippy," he said quietly. "Like a gentleman. She just didn't like it."

Anna nodded, her eyes tired and sad. "So what the hell are we going to do now?"

"Fight Miriam Shermer," Evan said evenly. "Cover every last one of her stupid, petty details and in one week shove them back up her ass where they came from."

Anna shook her head. "Evan, it's not enough time."

"I am not letting her win." Evan bit the words off one by one. "Come on, let's get out of here."

He took her arm and ushered her out of the building. Outside, a light breeze had sprung up. They walked the two blocks to his car, not saying a word. The crisp air bore the smell of autumn—rotting leaves, wood smoke and damp pavement. It was dark now, the brick sidewalk shadowed under trees that had not yet shed all their summer cloak.

Unlocking the door to his car, Evan helped her inside, then got in and started the engine. On the drive, her silence continued. It made him nervous. Anna was a Berzani and they were never quiet. He wished he knew what she was thinking. Somehow, he had to fix this mess for her—and for her parents. It was the least he could do.

Minutes later, he parked in the Berzanis' driveway.

"You don't have to get out," she said, gathering up her briefcase and reaching for the door handle.

"We can fight this, Anna," he said, touching her on the arm. "I have a few strings I can pull."

"Oh? There's more women you've slept with?" she asked, one eyebrow raised.

"People who owe me favors," he said, ignoring the taunt.

Anna sighed and closed her eyes for a moment. She looked tired, defeated and distant. Sitting with her, so close and yet so far apart, Evan felt lonely. It occurred to him that he was more alone in this minute than at any time that he could remember. Was that why he wanted so much to hold her? To kiss her? To ask forgiveness? After all the damage he had done, he doubted she would want his affection—or his apology.

Anna turned and looked at him. "I don't know what Pop's got up his sleeve. He's likely to do more harm than good."

"Jimmy will calm him down," Evan said. "I'll call him tomorrow. He'll help us keep Pop under wraps."

"I guess this means I'm not going back to San Francisco." Anna rubbed her temple.

A flutter of anticipation stirred in his chest: he would have her for one more week. The hope he felt made him pause. He only wanted time to settle things between them, that was all. Wasn't it?

"We're going to need somewhere to work," she said.

"Not here. Not with your father hanging around."

"What about the dealership?"

"I'd rather not. Too many interruptions for me." Evan was quiet for a moment, carefully contemplating the suggestion he was about to make. "We could use my apartment. I have an office with a large desk, high-speed internet, the works."

She looked at him for a long moment. He saw some of that Berzani determination restored to her eyes. Finally, she nodded, then opened the door. "Okay. What time?"

"How about nine o'clock?" He paused and looked at her

cautiously, unsure how personal he ought to get. "Unless you're not feeling so hot at that hour."

"Nine is fine," she said mildly. "My morning sickness is mostly gone. See you then."

Evan watched her walk to the front door and saw it close behind her. A light brightened the first-floor window. When a second light shone from one upstairs, he swallowed hard. She was in her bedroom now and he could imagine her there. He rested his forehead on the steering wheel for a minute, then sat back, put the car in gear and backed out of the driveway.

For one week, he was going to work with Anna. He knew that she would focus on the project and he would, too. But Evan also knew they had to deal with the chasm between them. Somehow he had to find a way to bridge that gap. He had to convince her that he could be a father, without making the mistake of becoming her husband.

Chapter Eleven

Anna listened to the tick and ping of the motor cooling as the chill air permeated the car. The weather had taken a definite turn toward winter today. The trees that lined the walkway swayed and shivered in the cold northwest wind. Leaves that had just turned bright shades of yellow and red skittered across the hood of the car, dancing and swirling in the breeze.

She checked her watch: five minutes past nine. She was late, but that didn't goad her. Eventually, she was going to have to get out of the car and knock on Evan McKenzie's door. Of course, it wasn't the actual knocking that was so daunting. It was the prospect of spending seven days with the man. Why did that seem like a Herculean task?

The answer was clear, though she wished she could deny it: her heart wanted to believe love was still possible. The idea of being alone with him in his house still made some perverse part of her soul sing. No matter how many times he crushed her with disappointment, this seed refused to die.

Anna didn't think of herself as an optimist. Before all this, she had thought of herself as a realist with cynical leanings. Now, she didn't know what she was. Her entire world had been picked up, shaken hard. The debris was still falling around her in unrecognizable patterns and her cynical realism often deserted her. Without it, she could not stifle the stupid, futile hope that Evan would change and come to love her.

Sighing, Anna put her head back against the seat. This was crazy. She had rehearsed this a million times already in her head. All night, she had told herself it was just work, a collaboration. For her parents' sake, she had to get through it. She reminded herself that she was here to do a job. Sitting in a cold car, wishing for the impossible, did no good.

Firmly resolved once more, Anna opened the car door and got out. From the backseat, she gathered her laptop and briefcase, then locked the door. She walked up the sidewalk, letting her professional eye take over as she looked around. Evan's building was as stunning a place as her mother's raves had promised. Each unit was three stories high with cantilevered decks hung from walls as if without support. The gray-washed cedar siding was punctuated with tall windows half-hidden by the trees. Nestled in banks of shrubbery, each condo was almost a separate private town house.

A walkway of pavers set in a chevron pattern led her to the front porch steps. With dread, Anna climbed them, but she knocked firmly on the door. Almost before she lowered her hand, the door swung inward. Evan stood there in gray trousers and a white shirt, a burgundy-paisley tie knotted firmly at his throat. All that was missing was the suit jacket to complete the ensemble. Under other circumstances, Anna might have laughed at his formal attire— they were just working in his home, after all—but like him, she had donned a skirt and blouse this morning, choosing the armor of business to set the correct mood.

"Hey," Evan offered without a smile.

"Sorry I'm late."

"No problem. I was just answering some e-mails from the office." He stepped aside and gestured her to enter. "Can I take your coat?"

Anna put her cases on a small table near the door and slipped out of her jacket. He put it in the closet, then grabbed her laptop bag and led the way down a short hall into the rest of his home. Picking up her briefcase, Anna followed silently.

For once, her mother had not exaggerated. Evan's home was like something from *House Beautiful:* airy, open and spacious. Two sofas in navy leather were arranged perpendicular to each other at the end of the room. A large coffee table, made from what appeared to be a ship's hatch, sat in front of them. There was the ubiquitous flat-screen television mounted on one wall, but the sound system was discreetly hidden in a cherry-wood cabinet beneath it. The walls were white, the floors maple with a clear varnish. The front wall was mostly glass, including French doors out onto a deck and beyond that, a magnificent view of the Chesapeake. It reminded Anna of her own panorama in San Francisco.

What surprised Anna was how finished and put together it all felt. There were beautifully framed pictures on the walls, a sculpture of a great blue heron in one corner, even the deck furniture coordinated.

"This is nice. Who did the interior?" she asked.

Evan had stepped into the kitchen, which was open to the rest of the room. With granite countertops and stainless-steel appliances, it was as much sculpture as functional work space.

"I did." He turned around with a bag of coffee in his hand and frowned. "You were expecting early man-cave?"

Anna shrugged. "I don't know many men with throw pillows on their sofas."

"Not Carl or your other architect friends?"

"Well, they're different," she said, fiddling with the handle of her bag. "They're paid to be coordinated."

He shook his head as he ground some beans and poured them into a coffee filter. He put the bag in the freezer, then rinsed and dried his hands. "There comes a time when even a dedicated bachelor has to stop living out of cardboard boxes and buy real furniture."

"So this is a recent conversion?" she asked, cocking her head to one side. It was a more personal question than she intended to ask, but her curiosity had gotten the better of her. Being in his apartment, she somehow felt closer to him than she ever had, perhaps even closer than the intimacy they had shared in San Francisco.

"Not recent. If I'm going to live somewhere, I move in completely. That means art, furniture and even matching dishes." Turning, Evan grabbed two mugs from a cupboard and held them up to her as evidence. Both bore the same pattern of scattered leaves on a white background. He smiled, just a slight lift of one side of his mouth, but it warmed his face. "Patrick's convinced I'm a freak."

Anna laughed. "If it weren't for Kate, Patrick would still be living on a boat and eating off paper plates. He's the freak."

"Do you want coffee?" he asked.

"Herbal tea, if you have it."

Anna stood watching Evan move around the kitchen, unsure of what to say—what to do—now. She felt like an intruder in his private domain. Tension lurked in the corners, ready to spring. She wondered if he felt the same.

Evan filled a glass teakettle with water and put it on the stove. "Why don't you go check out the office," he suggested. "It's up those stairs, down the hallway, to the right. I'll bring your tea when it's ready."

Grateful to escape, Anna grabbed her laptop case and climbed the steps he had indicated. At the top, she went down the hall. As she passed an open doorway, she couldn't resist peeking inside. It was a bedroom: obviously *Evan's* bedroom. She stopped, knowing she was snooping, but unable to turn around and leave.

A huge four-poster bed sat to the left, against the wall. Covered in a dark blue duvet, it looked soft and inviting. Anna swallowed as she imagined Evan lying there alone. Or with someone else. An image of his former girlfriend Kippy flashed into her head. Forcing her eyes away, she looked across the room to the windows that offered the same view as downstairs, drawing the eye.

There was a balcony here, too, furnished with a small table and a love seat that had a matching padded footstool. Evan had probably sat there many times with a companion. A woman, enjoying the afternoon sun, wearing his shirt and nothing else. She would snuggle next to him. Maybe they would share a glass of wine, kissing between sips. Then, when the sun went down and shadows filled the bedroom—

Anna cut off the painful thought. Backing up, she turned and fled the room with its unbearable scenes, continuing down the hall to what had to be the office. Facing the street, it didn't have the water-view of the other rooms, but was a pleasant space all the same. It was complete with an inlaid rosewood desk, two leather chairs, flat-screen monitor, file cabinets, printer, copier, everything ready for them to dive in and get to work.

Anna opened her laptop. As it came to life, she concentrated on the task at hand, pushing the rest aside. Work was her focus. That she had come to his home to do it was coincidental. She would ignore the bedroom down the hall, and forget about being the woman in Evan's life or in his bed. She was here to save the project and help her parents. They only had seven short days to make their case. Nothing else mattered. Not even these thoughts and feelings that someone less cynical than her might mistake for love.

EVAN STARED AT THE KETTLE without really seeing it, his hands braced against the edge of the stove. His attention followed Anna's footsteps on the hardwood floors above his head. They fell softly on the stairs, turned to go down the hall. She slowed, then stopped. He tensed, knowing that she was looking in his bedroom. One step more and silence.

Was she *inside* his bedroom? She must be. What was she looking at?

That question sent a bolt of heat through him, his body hardening with hunger. The urge to climb those stairs and coax her farther into that room was impossibly strong. Earlier, after he made the bed, Evan had almost closed the door. He had stopped himself. He never shut that door. Why close it today? What did he want to hide? Unable to answer his own questions, he had left it open.

Now he wished he had closed it: imagining her there, inside that room, was too much. Spinning around to the sink, he splashed cold water on his face and dried off with a hand towel. He could do this. For one week, they would work together. Judging by her garb, Anna meant to keep things as businesslike as he did.

The teakettle began to whistle. He turned off the burner, then poured hot water over the tea—mint that might soothe her stomach if it was upset this morning. Pouring himself coffee, he picked up the two mugs, took a deep breath and climbed the stairs. At the door to the office, Anna's back was to him as she leaned over her laptop. She turned and looked up as he entered.

"Find everything you need?" He set the mug next to her computer.

"Yes, thanks. I typed Madame Commissioner's list into my computer last night so we can dissect it. Here's a copy for you." She handed him a small memory stick.

He took it from her and looked at it, then popped it into his computer. Her brisk, get-down-to-work tone cleared the ground between them, but it still irked. Their conversation downstairs had recalled the evening they had spent together in San Francisco, an echo of the warmth and ease of being with her. He scolded himself for wanting to dance on the edge of danger, and sat in the chair opposite her.

"So, what should we tackle first?"

Anna pushed her laptop around so that he could see the screen. "I think half of her questions are just smoke. We've essentially answered them in the documentation already submitted. She just made them seem bigger by carping on the vanishing maritime community. I made some notes on how we might counter that."

"You must have stayed up late doing this," Evan said, keeping his eyes on the computer screen, hesitant to show his concern for her and the baby. She had never taken it too well over the phone.

Anna just shrugged. "Not too late."

"Well, don't push too hard." He slid a glance at her.

Anna lifted her mug and sipped her tea, effectively hiding her expression. "I couldn't sleep anyway."

Nodding, he agreed, "I was awake, too."

"There was a lot to think about."

He was silent for a moment, holding back the words on his tongue. He felt as if he was walking on eggshells, loud crackling sounding at every step. "I thought I could handle the zoning variance problem. I have a friend who works in city records who's willing to do some digging for us."

It was Anna's turn to say nothing. She sipped her tea again, then put the mug down before saying, "Sure. We could use help."

"So, I'll give him a call and see what he can find."

"Good."

Her reply sounded cool and flat to Evan's ears, attuned as he was to her every nuance. From what he could tell, all the warmth between them was gone now, banished to the time before things had gotten so complicated. He wished he could push back the clock, but knew it was a foolish desire. He could not change the past any more than it could change him or Anna Berzani.

Chapter Twelve

Anna pushed away from the computer and stood, leaving her shoes under the desk. Padding downstairs to the kitchen, she filled the kettle with water and put it on to boil. She pulled open the drawer where Evan kept tea, rummaging around until she found something that sounded good. It took a while since there were several blends to choose from. Every day, the stock of tea seemed to multiply. Mint, chai, lemon, chamomile, Lady Grey, three types of green—the selection would soon be too large for the drawer. Dropping a bag of lemon in her cup, she leaned against the counter, waiting for the water to heat.

It was strange to be in Evan's home when he wasn't there. Stranger still to feel so comfortable here. She was familiar now with the stereo and television controls, where he kept extra paper towels and the idiosyncrasies of the toaster—if she didn't push the button down firmly, it launched the bread ceiling-ward. After four days, it felt as if she had lived here forever. Odd how she could slip so seamlessly into a man's life and remain so distant from him.

The whistle sounded. Anna turned off the burner and poured the boiling water in her cup, the tea bag bobbing merrily. The proliferating tea was Exhibit A of the unspoken, odd connection between them. Evan never mentioned buying more tea for her; he just let her make the discovery.

And yesterday, he had seen her pull an apple out of her bag. Now there was a basket of fresh fruit on the counter which had not been there before.

He cared, he really did. She could believe that. Yet why did he not care enough to claim his child? He never mentioned the baby, but his every action told her it was on his mind. As the days progressed, Anna couldn't help feeling that if she weren't pregnant, if Evan did not feel so trapped, things might have worked out differently. He might learn to love her if she was not carrying his baby and all the commitment that a child entailed.

Sipping her tea, Anna stared out at the rain-swept day beyond the windows. Clouds glided low over the Bay and brought with them a steady drizzle. She cupped her hands around the warm mug, mulling over the situation. Two days ago, Evan had caught her napping on the sofa—a catnap for her strained eyes as well as her baby. He had offered his bed. When Anna refused, Evan had become irritable. He told her gruffly that the bed was more comfortable and she needed to take care of herself.

In his office, they worked well together. They laughed at each other's silly jokes. When he was in a funk, she could lift him out of it. When she was aggravated by the piles of documents, he could tell her a story about Patrick or her father and make her forget her frustrations. They *fit* together. Why, then, did he fight against them *being* together?

Sighing, she turned and walked back upstairs to the office. She didn't have time to waste on imponderables, not now. These questions, she felt sure, would never be answered. Especially since she couldn't get Evan to stand still long enough for her to ask them. He had nominated himself the mobile member of their team and was mostly out running errands and meeting with his mysterious contacts.

Whoever his friends were, they had certainly come through with a plethora of inside information. As a consequence, the office looked far less tidy and organized than it had that first morning. Rolled plans stood in the corners and stacks of papers lay on every available horizontal surface, as if a filing cabinet had exploded. Some of the piles waited to be read, others wanted returning to their rightful owner, while one pile needed to be copied so they could hand them to the planning commission.

Anna had also pulled some strings: her boss, Carl, had put her in contact with other architects in the area. They had offered plans of other completed projects that matched theirs in one way or another. Their defense was coming together and she was fairly certain they would be able to convince the commissioners—all except Ms. Shermer—of the value of the project. If only they could complete the work in time.

She returned to her seat in front of the computer and outlined her thoughts. The words came and she began to type. She made some presentation graphs showing peak volumes of traffic during the day. After that, she worked on a chart comparing the number of jobs and wages lost and gained by the project. Two hours later, she heard the alarm beep and a door close: Evan was home. Resisting the urge to go downstairs and greet him like a happy housewife, Anna kept her attention on the screen.

It did no good. The instant he appeared in the doorway of the office, she swiveled in her chair and greeted him with a grin and a warm, welcoming, "Hi!" Anna immediately cringed at herself. Why did she feel so bubbly when he walked back into her life?

Evan was still for a moment, his expression unreadable, then he smiled slightly. "Well, you're in a good mood.

Here," he said, dropping another stack of files on the desk in front of her. "This should cure it."

Anna flipped open the folder and looked at the top document, then back at Evan. His cool response had dampened her spirits more than another pile of paperwork to read. "What's this?"

"Our case for a zoning variance, I hope. I had to do some bargaining and begging to get it, but Craig thinks it'll convince the commission."

"That's good news," Anna said, her mood lifting once more.

Sitting in the other office chair, Evan stretched his legs out. He rubbed his hands over his face and sighed. "I hope so."

"You look tired." Anna tried to sound casual, but knew she failed.

He put an elbow on the armrest, and propped his chin on his fist. "I didn't get one of those catnaps you're so fond of."

"No one's stopping you now," she said tartly, as she blushed.

He had come home yesterday and found her sleeping in his bed. Despite her protests, Anna hadn't been able to resist the lure of lying there. It had been a mistake. Surrounded by his scent on the pillows and bedding, aching thoughts had kept her wide-awake, wishing he was with her. The penalty was so great that today she had given up and returned to the sofa.

He chuckled. "Too late. If I sleep now, I'll be up all night."

"That might happen anyway. We've only got the weekend to pull this together."

"We'll get it done. The city offices closed a half hour

ago," Evan said, looking at his watch. "I won't have to run around any more, so I'll be able to help you."

"Don't forget Ian and Mimi's going-away party tomorrow."

Evan dropped his head back and groaned. "Damn, I'd forgotten about that. Can we skip it?"

Anna shrugged. "*You* can. Pop told me he has a surprise for me, so I'm committed."

"Any idea what he's got planned?"

Anna shook her head. "I don't think I want to know. Probably something like a five-foot, papier-mâché statue of Michelangelo's *Pietà*."

Evan chuckled, then gusted another sigh and reached up to loosen his tie with one hand. The first button of his shirt followed. He closed his eyes, his head resting back against the chair. Anna drank in the sight of him, so still and relaxed. The urge to kiss his exposed throat, bared and vulnerable, was overwhelming. Only the weight of the unspoken matters between them kept her anchored to the chair.

Abruptly, he lifted his head and looked over at her. "You want a pizza? I missed lunch and I'm starved."

Anna looked at her watch. "No. I should go."

"Stay. Didn't you just say we were short on time?" He pulled out his cell phone and dialed a number. "What kind do you want?"

Lifting her hands in protest, she let them drop again. Why bother to fight? He was right. "Anything but shrimp."

"Not even dancing ones?" he asked, his eyes twinkling as he held the phone to his ear.

Anna remembered the conversation at the restaurant in Chinatown; it seemed a lifetime ago. Her heart picked up pace at the teasing light she saw so seldom in his eyes these days. "That was your caveat, not mine."

He laughed, then spoke over the phone. "Hey, I need a large everything, skip the shrimp and anchovies. Yeah... That's correct... Half an hour? Great." He hung up and tossed the phone on the desk. "I'm going to go change. Answer that if anyone calls."

Before Anna could speak, he was out of the office. She heard the door to his bedroom close, as she turned to her computer again.

Evan came back into the office minutes later. He was dressed in faded jeans and a blue sweatshirt that may at one time have had a logo on it. Now it had an indistinct pattern of white spots across the front. His feet were bare and his hair mussed, the golden strands sticking up. He looked absolutely delicious.

"I need a beer."

"Don't you want to go over this stuff?"

"It'll sound better with beer," Evan said as he walked out of the room.

A few minutes later, he returned holding two different bottles. He handed one to her. It was her favorite ginger-flavored iced tea. Another thoughtful, caring act from the man who would not marry her. "Thanks."

He sat and took a long swallow of his beer, then set it aside. "Okay, bring me up to date, chief."

Anna cleared her throat. As she explained what she had been doing over the past few days, she switched into business mode. It felt safe, soothing. Evan listened intently, asking pertinent questions. In a very short while, he was busy sifting through the stacks of paperwork for information. She felt at ease again. They took a break when the pizza came and dived back into work afterward. The evening flew by.

"Hey, here's the answer to the traffic study Miriam was

bitching about." He turned and handed a fat document to Anna.

She perused it, adding it to the growing pile and made a note on the computer. "Where did you get all this wonderful stuff?"

"People I know." Evan flipped through another file folder. "People they know."

"And how do you know all these...*people?*"

He shrugged and tossed the folder on their "potentially useful" pile. "I've sold them cars, or sold their parents cars, or raced on their boats, or...I don't know. It happens when you live here too long, I guess. You build up connections you don't even realize you have until you need them."

"The small-town life." Anna typed a few lines.

"I like it." Evan studied her. "You obviously don't."

Anna thought about that before she answered. Her hands stilled on the keyboard. "I don't think I'd mind it. Not now. When I left, I needed to get away from my family."

"Three thousand miles is definitely getting away."

"I don't know how you stand it. My parents don't know the meaning of 'butt out.'"

"Try having parents who don't butt in at all. My folks hardly seem to care what I do," Evan said.

"I'm envious."

"It's not as wonderful as you might think."

He had turned his back, so Anna couldn't read his face, but she kept staring at him. "I'm sure your parents care about you."

"Yeah, sure, they love me and all that. But they had a lot on their plates when I was a kid, with the divorce, then managing their own love lives." He kept flipping through the paperwork in the file he held. "They stopped telling me what to do a long time ago."

"So you let my parents do it instead?" Anna shook her head as she laughed a little. "That's nuts."

Evan tossed another file on the "completely useless" stack. "I don't know. The first time your dad yelled at me it felt like I was...like I mattered."

"Hmm. You must have felt very important around our house."

Evan chuckled. "Yeah, something like that."

Anna turned back to her computer and typed a few sentences, thinking about what he said. Over the years, she had never questioned why Evan had attached himself to her family and why his presence was never required at his own home.

"I guess your parents made me *feel* more loved than mine did," Evan said slowly. He laughed again, soft and low, with a trace of bitterness. "For a kid, discipline means someone cares. *My* parents were too busy yelling at each other to yell at me."

Anna's hands dropped to her lap as his words piqued her thoughts. She began to see how closely woven Evan was with her parents. Their opinion and approval mattered more to him than it did to her. Swiveling around in her chair, she studied him again. He was hunched over a chart spread out on the desktop. She needed to know if this was true, even if it violated the comfortable, safe mood they had established.

"Evan, is that why you don't want to tell them? About being the father?" she asked, probing gently. "Because you think they won't love you anymore?"

Evan lifted his head, looked out the window for a moment, and then his gaze met hers. "I know this is going to hurt them," he said. "I'd do anything if I could spare them that."

They stared at each other in silence for a long time.

Anna opened her mouth, then closed it. She needed to ask another question, except she wasn't sure she wanted to hear the answer. Maybe she was digging deeper than she ought.

"What?" he prompted. "Tell me."

"So it's not me?" she asked, daring to hope and searching his face for the truth.

He frowned. "You? I don't understand."

"It's not because you're ashamed of me?"

"Ashamed of you?" His shook his head and his frown deepened. "You asked that once before. I told you the answer."

"I didn't believe you. Not after that scene in my office with you, Pop and Carl. I mean, you won't marry me and maybe you don't want to marry anyone, but I felt that it *must* be me and—" Anna stopped and put a hand to her mouth. Where this confused litany was going, she didn't know. It revealed far too much and she wished she could take it back.

"I'm not ashamed of you, Annie. Not now. Not ever. I swear to you, that's the truth."

"If only I hadn't gotten pregnant." A single tear trickled down her cheek and she closed her eyes to stop the rest.

In moments, she was being drawn out of her chair and into Evan's arms. "Please, Annie. Don't cry."

"I'm sorry." In his embrace, the tears came faster.

She loved him. She could no longer feel angry. He could not love her, not the way she and her baby needed, but he was honest and he cared. He had never deceived her. He had deceived her parents, but not from shame.

"No, *I'm* sorry." Evan pulled her even closer, soothing a hand across her back. "The baby makes no difference. If I was going to marry anyone it would be you."

Being in his embrace was heaven. His soft words undid

her; it was not exactly what she wanted to hear, but he had given them freely and truly. Anna slipped her arms around his waist, leaning into him as she wept. Evan sifted his fingers through her hair, stroking the back of her neck when she hiccuped on a sob. Cupping her face with his hands, he urged her to look up at him. With his thumbs, he wiped away the wetness on her cheeks.

"Sweetheart, don't cry," he whispered, bending his head and brushing a soft kiss across her lips. He lifted his head, his eyes searching hers. "I never meant to hurt you."

Blinking back her tears, Anna saw worry, sorrow and tenderness in his green gaze. The need to give comfort— and receive it—had her sliding her hands up his chest to encircle his neck. She kissed him once, then twice, wanting more. Evan drew her close again and slanted his mouth over hers, delving deep, then pulling back.

"Please, Evan," she said, before he could speak. "Don't stop. I need you."

And she did. She needed his touch, his warmth and his love. Even if it was only for tonight.

"No. I won't hurt you again," he said, his voice rough.

"You won't," Anna said, standing on tiptoe to kiss him again. "I promise I won't hold you to anything. And this time, I promise I won't get pregnant."

He laughed a bit, but she read the hesitation in his face and pressed her body to his in a sensual slide. Desire conquered indecision as he lowered his lips to hers, hot and demanding. Anna's heart began to race as passion rose between them. Lifting her in his arms, Evan carried her across the hall to his bedroom. Laying her on the bed, he gently covered her with his hard body, kissing her fiercely.

Anna drowned in his touch, his taste. She had wanted this for so long, yet feared that she would never be this close to him again. Running her hands under his sweatshirt, she reached bare skin. His muscles bunched and rippled as he drew her tightly against his chest. Their mouths melded, tongues dancing in concert as they delved deeper and deeper.

Suddenly, he rolled over, so that she lay on top of him. Her legs fell to each side of his, bringing them into intimate contact. Anna moaned, a gasp of pleasure that would not be contained. As if in answer to her call, Evan's palms smoothed over her thighs to the edge of her skirt, then under it. Grasping her bottom, he arched upward, pressing his erection to her.

The clothes between them were a hindrance she couldn't stand a second longer. She needed to *feel* him again, her skin to his. Anna pushed against his chest and he loosened his grip. Evan's eyes held a question—a concern—she didn't bother to answer. Rising to her knees, she straddled him and fumbled for the buttons on her blouse. He sat up, too, and pulled his sweatshirt over his head.

The sight of his chest distracted her from undressing. Reaching out, she slid her palms over the hair-roughened skin. He swallowed, Adam's apple bobbing, as she stroked over the hard planes and downward. Anna kissed his throat, then nipped him gently. His scent filled her head, the citrus tang of pure Evan. Smiling in anticipation, she leaned back a little, finding her buttons again.

Evan followed her forward, kissed her and pushed her fingers aside. "Let me."

First he bit her lower lip, before laving the spot with his tongue. Anna shivered when he nibbled at her earlobe. Next came a line of fire as his mouth worked its way down her throat. When he finally got to her blouse, it was slow work as he stopped to kiss her between each button. It was wonderful, but frustrating: she wanted his bare skin on hers even more now.

"You're taking too long," she said with a breathy laugh.

"It's called anticipation." His voice was low and rasping, shivering across her nerves like a caress.

"What do you think I've been doing for thirteen years?"

Evan threw back his head and laughed loudly. "*You?* What about me? You've been driving me crazy."

Anna slid her hands up Evan's chest and around his neck. "Prove it," she said with a teasing smile. "Show me how crazy."

Evan grinned, his eyes glittering with intent. Carefully, he took one side of her blouse in each hand and yanked. Buttons flew, one pinged on a lamp and landed on the end table, another ricocheted off a painting and fell to the floor. "How's that?" he asked.

"It's a good start."

With a laugh, he scooped her closer and put his lips to hers once again. Moments later, her shirt slipped off her shoulders. He dealt with her bra just as quickly. Lying back, he drew her down on top of him again. Anna threaded her fingers into his hair, holding his mouth to hers as he worked her skirt down over her hips and off.

Shifting to one side, Evan cupped one of her breasts, taking the nipple into his mouth. The sensuous slide of his tongue against skin made her writhe in need. He transferred his attention to her other breast, pushed her on her back again and glided a hand down over her belly, slowing and coming to a stop over the slight mound there. Anna held her breath, fearing his hesitation.

"Can we do this?" he asked against her lips.

"Oh, yes," Anna said on a sigh. "Please."

Gently, he rubbed a circle over their child, acknowledging its presence. Then he continued downward to slip his fingers under her panties and touch her most intimate flesh. The tears that rose to Anna's eyes were quickly burned away in the heat of her passion for this man. Her nails bit into his shoulders as he drew her underwear off, then stroked her to the brink of pleasure.

Anna groaned when Evan took his hand away. Opening her eyes, she saw him wrenching open the buttons on his jeans and shoving them down and off his long legs. His erection sprang free and she couldn't resist reaching down to touch him. Evan fell back with a gasp that quickly turned to a moan. His shoulders rose from the bed as the muscles across his stomach tensed.

Running a hand over that hard, resilient surface, Anna traced a lingering trail from there down one thigh. Evan grabbed her wrists and pressed her back to the bed with a growl. His mouth came down on hers, hard and demanding. Anna joyously welcomed his naked desire. Rising above her, Evan fitted himself to the softness of her body and entered her with one urgent thrust.

It was as magical as the first time, a complete melding of two bodies into one. His grip on her wrists loosened. Meshing his fingers with hers, he locked their hands together as he began to move against her. Building the pace slowly, he drove them both toward completion. She tilted her hips, drawing him deeper inside. He responded by increasing the tempo. Anna was lost; all she knew was Evan and the intense pleasure he made her feel.

Opening her eyes, she gazed up into his face. The hot, hungry desire she saw there fed her own. Anna was spinning out of control. He brushed her lips with his just as she tipped over the edge into ecstasy so intense she thought her heart would burst. Arching her back, she strained against the bonds of their joined hands. A cry rose from her throat, joined by his hoarse shout.

For a moment, Anna thought she would fly to pieces, but Evan's grip held her firmly anchored to the bed. Safe forever. Unchecked by anger or ignominy, her heart flooded with love and whispered the words aloud into the silence between them. His fingers tightened on hers. A tear fell from her eye, but this time it was from happiness. She would never need anything more than this. Never.

Chapter Thirteen

A rain shower had passed through sometime after midnight, kicking the wind up. The moon, appearing from behind the clouds, washed light across the hardwood, just touching the end of the bed. Evan lay relaxed under the covers, watching the bright beam arc slowly across the room. As tired as he was, he should be asleep, but his mind would not settle. That was due to the woman lying next to him.

With her back to him, Anna lay curled on her side, a warm weight against his hip. Her hair spilled in a shadowed cloud across the pillow. The curls tickled his cheek as he turned his head to look at her, their sweet floral scent filling his nostrils. The urge to roll over and fit himself to the curve of her body one more time was strong. He had satisfied that craving more than once, waking her with slow caresses that led to more. She had done the same, delighting him with her passion and open warmth.

This time, Evan let her sleep. She needed rest and so did the baby. He remembered touching the evidence of the life they had created. Oddly, he had felt no panic, just awe and an incredible spike of hunger to be inside her again. Every time he made love to Anna Berzani he was amazed. And here he was, contemplating another go, despite his fatigue and a nagging recognition that he was getting in way too deep with this woman.

I love you.

Had she said that? Her voice had been a whisper of sound, barely heard over the pounding of his heart. He had listened intently, but she had not said any more, except for the moans and sighs of pleasure.

Did he love her? He knew he liked having her around his house. She was easy to work and play with: funny, intelligent, undemanding, beautiful. They were incredible in bed together. He wanted her and she wanted him, that was clear.

Was that love? And if it was, how long would it last?

The questions roused him from bed. He grabbed his clothes from the floor, put them on and quietly left the bedroom. Downstairs, he opened the door to the deck and stepped outside. The night air was cold, but he hardly noticed as he leaned his elbows on the rail. The dark, calm water soothed him, but dawn would come soon. Evan doubted that anything would be clearer in the light of a new day.

I love you.

He clenched his fingers on the cold metal as her words flooded him again. Part of him wanted to believe that Anna *had* indeed said it. Another bigger, stronger part was already running away in panic. He didn't love her. He couldn't. He was incapable of loving anyone. He might feel something like love right now, but all too soon the restlessness would set in and he would crave freedom. When that happened, he would hurt Anna even more. Their child, too. He had paid the price for a father who could not be tied to a wife and child; he would *not* do that to his own.

The sky had started to lighten in the east; birds were calling to one another. Evan rubbed his hands over his face, pressed his fingertips into his tired eyes and went back inside. In the kitchen, he looked up, as if he could see Anna through the floor between them. He couldn't go back to bed and compound this mistake.

Instead, he scooped up his keys from the counter where he had tossed them last night. At the door, he pulled tennis shoes out of the closet and shoved his bare feet into them. He would go to the club, change clothes there and go for a long run. The exercise would clear his head and maybe put an end to his selfish, hopeless desire. He wanted Anna Berzani, but there was no use kidding her or himself. It wasn't going to last. Leopards never changed their spots. Why should Evan McKenzie think he could change his?

THE PARTY WAS IN FULL SWING. About three-dozen people had come to wish Ian and Mimi bon voyage. Anna chatted and laughed with friends she knew and some strangers she didn't. She played with Patrick's daughter, Beth, for a while. She helped Elaine set out food and argued with Jeannie about how much balsamic vinegar to put into the dressing. She avoided her father, who earlier had asked when she had gotten home last night. She had led him to believe she had come in late, then gone out again early. He grumbled about the hours she was keeping. She wasn't about to tell him she hadn't come home at all.

Luckily, she had slipped into the house undetected and changed out of the large T-shirt she had borrowed from Evan's drawer. Her blouse was unwearable and more incriminating than the T-shirt. She had collected the scattered green buttons from Evan's bedroom, but had no needle and thread to sew them back on with. In a fit of pique, she had left them on his nightstand as a reminder of their passion.

Would he remember her otherwise?

Evan had been gone when she awoke. Anna had dressed and worked on her computer for a while, trying to ignore the clock ticking off the minutes. Maybe he had gone to get coffee and bagels. Maybe something came up at the dealership and he would call her. Maybe he had abandoned her and was hiding until she packed up and got out of his house.

She had promised not to hold him to anything. He wasn't in love with her. He had told her time and again he wouldn't marry her. She had *promised* herself she would simply accept his passion for as long as he was willing to give it. No one had deceived anyone. Still, Anna blinked back tears as she poured another glass of lemonade. It was hard work keeping anyone here from guessing how heartbroken she felt.

Taking her glass to the living room, Anna sat on the sofa next to Mimi. Her friend greeted her with a smile.

"I hear your dad's got a big surprise for you."

Anna rolled her eyes. "I'm hoping it's perishable."

"Well, if it's not, how often do they visit?"

"Often enough. And he keeps track of things like that. Did you see the olive press he gave Patrick and Kate for a wedding gift? Big, useless *and* they can't get rid of it since it's a family *heirloom*," Anna said, ticking off points on her fingers.

Mimi burst into laughter as Ian walked up. He sat on the other side of his wife, curving an arm around her. The affectionate gesture, one that spoke of love and trust, almost made Anna start to cry again. Ian's brows lowered as he looked at her.

"What's wrong, sis?"

"I'm going to miss you," Anna said hastily.

"You can come see us," he said, his face clearing. "Anytime."

Patrick came over, carrying Beth. "Where's McKenzie?"

Anna tried to look nonchalant and shrugged. "How should I know?"

"You've been working with him," Ian said. "How's that going? You need any help?"

"What? Evan *working?*" Patrick asked with a chuckle. "I doubt that."

"He's done most of it," Anna said with a snap, glaring at Patrick. "I'm just assembling the pieces."

She bit her lip when both her brothers looked at her with raised eyebrows. A gleam in Ian's eyes made Anna squirm. She shot a glance at Mimi who gave a slight shake of her head.

The loud ringing of a ship's bell spared Anna from saying any more. At the far end of the room, Antonio was gleefully tugging the rope on the clapper, interrupting all conversation. He had prepared a welcome speech for the party, a long-winded eulogy to his brave son, his stalwart daughter-in-law and her clever son who would soon be leaving for far-flung ports. Everyone clapped in the appropriate pauses and Antonio concluded with a toast in their honor.

Just when everyone supposed he was finally finished, Antonio rang the bell again. "I have another announcement. Anna Maria, please come here."

Anna took a deep breath and squared her shoulders. Prepared for any embarrassment, she went to her father's side.

He put a hand on her shoulder and made her face the gathering. "I want you all to know, that my little girl, the gem of my heart, she is going to have a baby!"

Most of the gathering knew this already, but they all raised their glasses or applauded.

"She has made her mother and I so happy. To mark the occasion I have a special gift that I want to give." Antonio disappeared into the kitchen for a moment and came out with what looked like a large wooden box.

Anna couldn't believe what she was seeing. With a hand that trembled, she reached out and touched the satiny surface. It was a cradle made of cherry. The headboard was carved in an intricate swirl of curlicues, with delicate flowers and leaves running along the top. The footboard had a matching design. Inside was a soft pad covered with dark blue velvet.

Her gaze flew to her father's and her voice came out as a squeak. "Oh, Pop!"

"For my newest grandchild," Antonio said, putting the cradle in her arms.

Anna stroked the wood, fingering the beautiful carvings. Tears rose and ran unchecked down her cheeks. It was the loveliest thing she had ever seen. Antonio had handcrafted similar cradles for each of his grandchildren. She and her father had fought so much lately, it was a gift of the heart Anna had never expected to receive. Yet here it was, proof that, despite their differences, he really did love her. Awkwardly shifting the cradle to one arm, Anna put a hand over her face and sobbed.

Ian came over and offered her a handkerchief. Mimi patted her on the shoulder. Anna wiped her face, but was unable to speak.

"Why is she crying so?" Antonio asked Elaine, who had also come to Anna's side.

"Hush, dear. She just appreciates the gift."

Looking up at her father, Anna struggled to find the words to express her feelings.

Antonio frowned, his arms crossed over his chest. "She is tired. Evan is making her work too hard."

Anna sucked in a breath to disagree just as Evan walked in the door.

"Speak of the devil. Here he is," Patrick said, punching him in the arm. "Where've you been, McKenzie?"

"I...I had to stop at the dealership," Evan said. He had frozen near the door, his eyes wide as he took in the tableau encircling Anna. "What's wrong?" he asked.

"This is your fault," Antonio said, pointing a finger at him. "What do you have to say for yourself?"

The room got quiet. Evan flinched as if all the eyes in the room were piercing him with darts. "I'm sorry, Pop. It was an accident. But I told Anna I'd support her and the baby. Any way I can."

Anna closed her eyes for a moment, then opened them and looked at Evan again.

"Oops." This came from Mimi, who clapped a hand over her mouth. She looked at Anna, horror mingled with amusement in her eyes.

"What do you mean *take care of the baby?*" Antonio asked, his voice puzzled.

"Oh, my goodness." Elaine held a hand to her cheek. She had obviously put the pieces together.

"What the *hell* are you talking about, McKenzie?" Patrick said with a frown, his voice rising. Beth started to cry when he shouted. Kate took their daughter from Patrick's arms and bounced her, trying to calm her down.

"You've *got* to be kidding," Jeannie said as she sat with a plop on the nearest chair.

A light had dawned in Evan's eyes as he realized he might have confessed to his deed prematurely. There was nothing Anna could do. She wrapped her arms around the cradle and hung on to it.

Antonio finally seemed to grasp the significance of Evan's words. He turned on the younger man with a roar. "*You* are the father of Anna's child?"

Evan stood tall. He was white-faced, but not backing down. "Yes, sir. I am."

Anna shoved the cradle at Mimi and slipped past her father to stand in front of Evan. "Calm down, Pop." Her order only produced a stream of Italian, harsh and furious. "I didn't tell you, either, because—"

"It was not for you alone, Anna Maria." Antonio's voice was alarmingly quiet now. "Evan is a man. He must act like one."

"Pop, I love you. But this is between me and Evan."

"It is not!" Patrick's face was livid. "This affects the whole family."

"Shut up, Patty," Ian said. "It's not your battle."

Antonio ignored them all and demanded of Evan, "Are you going to marry my daughter?"

Evan stepped around Anna. "I don't—"

"Stop shouting, Tonio," Elaine said as Beth's cries rose once again. "You're scaring your granddaughter."

"I will not have this!" Antonio shook a finger at his wife, then pointed it at Evan. "He must do the right thing."

"Pop, please," Anna said, putting a hand to her head where a killer headache had blossomed. Turning to Evan, she said, "Let's just adjourn to the kitchen, okay?"

Anna took a few steps, then turned when she realized no one was following her. Her eyes widened when she saw Evan, one knee on the floor. As she stared, a trickle of sweat rolled down the side of his face. She frowned. "What's wrong? Are you feeling faint?"

He shook his head and wet his lips. "Anna Berzani?" he asked, slowly and clearly. "Will you marry me?"

The words dropped like stones from his lips and rippled to the far corners of the living room. Her father let out a satisfied grunt while her mother gasped. Ian shook his head as Mimi rested her forehead against his shoulder. Kate took

Patrick's hand. Jeannie hugged herself and looked worried. Others in the room were likewise touched or discomfited by the request.

Anna felt as if she had been hit with a sledgehammer. Her ears rang and her head spun. She stared at Evan for a moment longer. "Why? Because my father wants you to?"

"No. Because you want it," he said, looking at her with shaky, uncertain, lusterless eyes. The prospect of marriage had killed the spark that usually shone there.

She shook her head. "No." She hugged herself, rubbing her arms to try and get rid of the icy chill that seemed to creep over her skin. "No, Evan McKenzie, I won't marry you."

"What? I thought… Are you sure?"

"Duty isn't love. And I love you too much to force you into this."

The words made him flinch worse than before and a flush rose up to stain his cheeks. His eyes met hers again. She could see the ache she felt reflected in the green gaze.

"I'm sorry, Annie," he said softly. "I never meant to hurt you." With that, he stood and walked out of the house.

When the latch clicked, Anna released the breath she had been unconsciously holding. Elaine came to her, embracing her without a word. Letting her head droop onto her mother's shoulder, she clung tightly. Despite the comforting arms and the family and friends in the room, Anna felt so completely alone. This time her heart would not bounce back. This time, she knew the truth: it was over. The pain was overwhelming and tears began to fall.

Chapter Fourteen

The scent of frying bacon wafted through the warm kitchen. A beam of sunlight spread over the table, brightening the whole room. Anna stood in the doorway, absorbing the familiar scene: her father reading the Sunday paper, her mother cooking, the radio playing softly. She had taken moments like this for granted too many times—even been irritated by their sameness. This morning it seemed infinitely dear, a haven from all the turbulence life had thrown at her. For the moment, she could almost believe that yesterday had never happened.

Elaine threw a smile over her shoulder. "Good morning, dear."

"Morning, Ma." Anna slipped into a chair at the table.

Her father looked up from his newspaper. His eyes narrowed as he scanned her features. "Good morning. Did you sleep well?"

"Not especially," Anna said. She could lie, but her swollen, red eyes gave it away.

Antonio set the paper aside. "I will talk to Evan."

"No, Pop." Anna reached a hand to him across the table. He took it, his grip calloused, but gentle. "I know you think we should get married, but that's not the answer for either of us."

"A child needs two parents."

"And he or she *will* have two parents," she countered and squeezed his hand. "Evan will be a father, he just won't be my husband."

"Evan is a fool," Antonio said indignantly. He frowned and shook his head, letting out a heavy sigh. "And he has wronged us."

Anna felt a pang of guilt at his words. The damage done to Evan's relationship with her father was partly her fault. "Please, try not to be too hard on him. Evan's never lied to me about who he is, or what he wants." Anna laughed a little, but it was more sadness than humor. "I may have lied to *myself* about him, but he's always been straight up with me."

"You are too generous, Anna Maria," her father said, shaking his head. "That is one of your strengths. But now it is a weakness."

Anna shrugged. "What can I do? I love him."

"He does not deserve your love."

"You've always taught me that love forgives."

Elaine brought over a cup of tea, set it on the table and kissed her daughter on the top of the head. She smoothed a strand of hair behind Anna's ear and put a hand under her chin, tilting her face up.

"Don't worry, dear," her mother said with a faint smile. Her gray eyes were full of concern. "It will work out somehow."

Anna sighed, a wobbly breath that held more tears. She swallowed them back before they could fall. "I hope so."

Elaine hugged her, then went back to the stove. As she cooked, she kept up a steady stream of chatter.

Anna sipped her tea, not saying anything. She let her mother's words flow past her ears without absorbing any. It was a familiar sound, soothing to her tired, troubled heart. Antonio grunted occasionally. Whether that meant he agreed with what she said, or was simply pretending he had heard it, Anna had never figured out. Whichever the case, the routine worked for them.

Elaine set three plates of bacon and eggs on the table, adding a basket of freshly baked biscuits. Butter and home-made jam completed the repast.

"Do you still plan to leave on Tuesday, Anna?" her mother asked when they had all started in on breakfast.

Anna buttered a biscuit and reached for the strawberry jam. "Yes. I've got to get back to my office."

Elaine pursed her lips. "When will you be back?"

"I have no idea. The delay on your project has put me way behind schedule. No more vacations for this girl." Anna glanced at the clock over the stove. She still had work to do before her second presentation to the planning commission.

Elaine stopped, staring at her daughter, coffee cup halfway to her mouth. "Surely you'll be home at Christmas?"

"Of course she will." Antonio patted Elaine's hand.

Anna took a bite of eggs and chewed slowly. It was strange: she found herself wishing she could stay here with her parents longer. There was an ease to being with them now, the rubbing that had once irritated her felt soothing, as if someone had polished and oiled the rough surface between them. It didn't even bother her that her father had assumed she would be here.

"Definitely for Christmas," Anna promised.

"Good." Elaine drank from her cup, then set it aside. "The nicest young man just bought the optical store on Crestmount. I think you and he would get along very well."

Anna's mouth dropped open, hardly able to believe her own ears.

Antonio cleared his throat. "Perhaps it is too soon to discuss this."

"Why?" Elaine blinked at both of them, looking astonished. She turned to her husband first. "Anna is single and so is he. I don't see why they shouldn't go on a date."

"But Evan—"

"If he has a problem with it, he can speak up," Elaine said sharply, interrupting her husband. "Anna can't put her life on hold forever."

"Don't you think my pregnancy might hinder my dating life?" Anna asked.

Elaine waved a dismissing hand. "I told him about your condition," she added in a confiding tone. "He didn't even bat an eyelash."

The triumph on her mother's face was too much to bear. Anna started to laugh. She looked at her father, who chuckled as he leaned over and kissed his wife on the cheek. Elaine shook her head, but her smile was still smug. Wiping tears—of laughter this time—away from her eyes, Anna picked up her plate and put it in the sink. Despite their differences, she appreciated her parents as she never had before. They did love her. It recompensed some of the pain.

THE DOORBELL RANG, BUT Evan ignored it. There was no one he wanted to talk to today. Maybe no one he wanted to talk to *ever*. The bell rang again. He turned up the volume on the stereo. It sounded a third time and didn't stop. Even the music wouldn't drown out the incessant noise. Swearing, he flipped the stereo off with the remote and stomped down the hall to the front door.

He yanked it open, ready to do battle. "What!"

Ian stood on the front step, hands in the pockets of his hoodie. "Hey."

Anger left Evan in a rush, leaving an empty void. "Aren't you supposed to be sailing to Bermuda?"

Ian shrugged. "We delayed till after the big meeting. Can I come in?"

Evan stood back, closing the door behind his friend. At least he *thought* Ian was still his friend. After yesterday, he couldn't be sure. Ian walked into the living room and Evan followed.

"You want something to drink?"

"I wouldn't say no to a beer."

Evan went to the refrigerator and pulled out two bottles, opened them and passed one over. Ian took it and sipped. Pulling out a chair, he sat at the table. Evan leaned against the bar, too tense to sit.

"You look like hell," Ian observed.

"Thanks."

"How are you feeling?"

With a shrug, Evan paced over to the windows, staring out sightlessly. "I'll live."

"That's a depressing prognosis."

"You want me to tell you I'm killing myself over your sister?" Evan asked, his voice hard. "I'm not."

"I'd rather you told me you were in love with my sister."

"Sorry. I'm not that, either."

Ian was silent.

Evan sighed. "Look." He turned around and faced the other man. "How many girlfriends have I had over the years?"

"You're asking me?" Ian snorted a laugh. "Well, let's see. First I'd have to know how many available women there are in a hundred-mile radius of this town."

"Smart-ass," Evan muttered. "I've had a lot. That's my

point. I've never stayed with one of them longer than six months. Is that what you want for her?"

Ian cocked his head to one side. "Have you ever stopped to think that the reason you've never had a long-term girl-friend is because you've been waiting for Anna?"

Evan rolled his eyes. "You're nuts."

"Think about it," Ian said, pinning him with a stern gaze. "You've wanted her since she was sixteen. You couldn't have her, so you used other women to distract yourself. They never meant anything because Anna's the one you *really* want. You were marking time."

"She's been legal a long time, Ian."

"Yeah, but she's also your best friend's sister," Ian said, drinking his beer. "That put her off-limits, too."

The doorbell rang again before Evan could counter this drivel. Ian had been bitten by love and had stopped making sense, he thought as he walked down the hallway. When he opened the door, Evan was shocked from his whirling thoughts again. Patrick stood on the stoop.

"Hey." Patrick's greeting was stiff, without his usual heartiness. His eyes were shadowed and wary beneath the brim of his ball cap.

"Hey."

"Can I come in?"

"Uh, yeah. Why not?" Evan stood back, letting Patrick walk past him. "Ian's here."

"He beat me to it." Patrick followed Evan down the hall.

Ian saluted his brother with his beer. "Hey, Patty," he said cheerfully. "Come to help me pound McKenzie to a bloody pulp?"

Without a word, Evan got out another beer, opened it and handed it over. Patrick took it, but seemed as rest-less as Evan. He prowled over to the windows and stood looking out, his back to the other men. Evan picked up his own bottle and downed half the contents in a gulp. Patrick turned and came back to stand in front of Evan.

"I *should* beat you senseless," he said, his eyes blazing with anger. He took a swig of beer. "You deserve it."

Evan set his drink down carefully on the bar, ready for anything. "Probably."

"Probably?" Patrick's voice rose. "You knock up my sister, keep it a secret for two months and you think you *probably* deserve to get beat up?"

"Anna didn't tell us, either," Ian said mildly. "You going to beat her up, too?"

"This isn't about Anna. It's about us. Him and me," Patrick said to Ian impatiently. He turned back. "We've been friends for years, Evan. Why didn't you come to me?"

"What would you have done?" Evan shot back. "As I recall, you were ready to jump on whoever was responsible. Beat the bastard up first, ask questions later."

"I would have been pissed off. Sure, but I'd have gotten over it," Patrick shouted. "We're *friends,* dammit. *Best* friends. Or so I thought."

As he spoke the last words, his voice dropped. Evan knew his biggest crime in all of this mess had been in not telling anyone what was going on. He hadn't wanted to disappoint anyone, but he had managed to hurt them more with his silence. He ran a hand through his hair, then looked directly at Patrick.

"I'm sorry. I didn't …" His voice trailed off, his thoughts scattered. He could only repeat, "I'm sorry."

"Yeah, you ought to be," Patrick said in a growl. "Sometimes, McKenzie, you are the biggest jerk on the face of the planet."

"And sometimes you are," Ian said to Patrick. "That's why you two get along so well."

"Do you have a point?" Patrick demanded of his brother.

"You've had your say. Lay off him. He's got enough problems."

Patrick walked over and pulled out a chair at the table. Sitting, he shrugged out of his jacket, then pushed his cap back on his head. "You look like shit," he said to Evan.

"So I've heard." Evan picked up his beer and took a drink. "I didn't sleep much last night."

"You going to try to get Anna to change her mind?" Patrick asked.

"Don't be stupid," Ian said, picking at the label on his beer bottle. "McKenzie doesn't want to get married."

"Why'd he ask her then?"

"What would *you* have said with Pop bearing down on you like that?" Ian said drily.

"There's a point," Patrick said, nodding slowly. "How come you don't want to marry her?"

"He doesn't love her," Ian said before Evan could answer.

"You want me to go upstairs so you two can discuss this alone?" Evan asked irritably.

"Nah. Bring your beer over and sit down."

Patrick pushed another chair out with his foot. Reluctantly, Evan did as he was told. He didn't want this inquisition, but these were his two closest friends. He needed them. But they were Anna's brothers, too. How could he expect them to help him?

"How do you know you don't love her?" Patrick asked Evan.

"How do you know you do love someone?" Ian asked in a musing tone.

"Please." Patrick rolled his eyes. "No amateur philosophy."

"I just know I don't," Evan said, ignoring the byplay between the brothers.

Ian shook his head. "You love her."

"I do not!" Evan sat back, glaring at the two men. "Whatever crazy—"

"Do you think about her all the time?" Ian asked leaning forward and punctuating each question with a tap on the table. "Have trouble eating or sleeping when she's not around? Do you want to do stupid little things for her, just to make her happy? Do you do anything to keep her from leaving? Can't wait to see her again when she *does* go?"

Evan was silent. He didn't like the fact that Ian's questions hit uncomfortably close to home. He *had* felt that way about Anna this week. Life had quickly started to feel incomplete and empty now that she wasn't around. Lack of sleep was just one symptom. Crossing his arms over his chest, he tried to keep his face blank.

Patrick drank the last of his beer and lifted an eyebrow at Ian. "You want another?"

"Yeah. Get McKenzie one, too. He needs it." Ian kept his gaze locked on Evan. "Not answering is as good as admitting it's true."

"So why not marry her?" Patrick asked bringing three bottles back to the table and setting them down.

"What is the deal with marriage? Just because you're both married doesn't mean *I* should be. For Pete's sake, it isn't the answer to everything!" Evan slapped his hands on the table, glaring at the two brothers. Neither looked impressed. "No matter what you say, I am *not* getting married."

"Just because your parents screwed it up doesn't mean you will," Patrick said, pointing his bottle at Evan.

"Patty, they didn't screw up, they *exploded* that marriage and I happened to be standing in the blast zone." Evan shook his head slowly back and forth. "I am not putting my kid through that."

"So don't. Get married and don't get divorced."

Evan snorted. "Nobody sticks around forever, least of all me."

"I don't get this," Patrick said. "You think Kate and I will get divorced, or Ian and Mimi?"

"I didn't say that."

"Yeah, you did." Patrick pushed his beer aside and leaned his elbows on the table. "Nobody ever said any marriage was perfect, Evan. Everybody fights and it can get ugly sometimes. Shit, when Kate and I go head-to-head, it's like I'm channeling Ma or Pop."

"Can I bring popcorn and watch sometime?" Ian asked with a grin.

Patrick ignored him, locking his eyes on Evan. "You don't get a guarantee. All you get is work, every day."

"That's quite the endorsement," Evan said drily. "Gee, let me rethink my position."

"You should rethink it," Patrick agreed. "Because what you *do* get is amazing. Love and trust and friendship and laughter, the list is endless. It's the hardest thing I've ever done in my life and at the end of every day, I hope I get a chance to do it again tomorrow."

When Patrick finished his sermon, silence fell over the room. Evan didn't know what to say. He just shook his head. It sounded so glorious but he could not make them see. He didn't have the Berzani gene for lifetime commitments. All he had was the McKenzie gene, the one his father had passed on for loving and leaving.

Ian finished his beer and stood. "Well, I guess my job here is done. Oh, except Anna asked me to pick up her laptop and some paperwork for tomorrow. She said there's still a lot of work to be done before the meeting."

"I did most of it last night," Evan said, standing and rubbing two fingers into his tired eyes. The beer had kicked in and made his already fuzzy brain worse. "Since I couldn't sleep anyway. Tell her…tell her I'll finish it today and I'll drop it by the house in the morning."

"Better if you call me and I'll come pick it up," Ian said, his expression neutral.

Evan looked at him and heard what he wasn't saying. "She doesn't want to see me?"

Ian shrugged. "Why would she?"

The words hit like a punch in the solar plexus. "I guess I don't know."

Evan led the way up the stairs and gave Ian the laptop in its case.

Patrick looked around the messy office with the stacks of paper and the rolls of drawings. "You really put some effort into this, didn't you? I had no idea it was so involved."

"We want to make sure it happens." Evan paused. "For your parents."

"They'll appreciate it," Ian said.

"If they ever speak to me again," Evan added flatly.

"How long does Pop hold a grudge?" Patrick asked. "A couple of explosions, then it's over."

Evan wasn't so sure, especially in this case. This was not some schoolboy prank that deserved a paternal tongue-lashing. This was a serious, heart-deep wound. He followed the two men back downstairs and to the door. Letting them out, he stood on the front porch as they walked away. But Ian turned back a few steps as if he had forgotten something.

"You've kept a flame burning for Anna for twelve years, Evan. That should tell you something about your ability to be faithful."

"Desire isn't love."

"Maybe not, but it's a damn good place to start." With that, Ian turned and caught up with his brother.

Sighing tiredly, Evan went back inside and shut the door. All he had done lately was hurt people. Anna, Antonio, Elaine, Patrick, Ian: another endless list. Ian had obviously forgiven him, Patrick would eventually, but damage had been done to their relationship. As for Antonio and Elaine? Evan sat on the sofa and stared blankly out the window. He had lost the only real family he knew.

He laid his head back and closed his eyes. At least he had proven himself right: just like his father, he had abandoned those who mattered most to him. The look on Anna's face when he had asked her to marry him flashed in his mind. She was right, too. He didn't love her. Thank God for that. If he did love her, just think of the damage he could have done.

Chapter Fifteen

"Oh, look! There's Claire!" Elaine patted Anna's arm. "I'll just go say hello."

Anna turned and saw Mimi's parents, Claire and George Green, strolling down the aisle toward them. She waved and smiled, but did not leave her chair. She needed a few minutes alone to compose herself. Physically, she was prepared for the coming meeting, emotionally was another story.

Facing forward, Anna gazed at the same navy-skirted table arrayed with microphones she had seen a week ago. The same two flags hung limp behind it. The same podium stood off to the left on the same dull, gray carpet. Yet everything in Anna's life had changed. Amazingly, it had taken only seven days for her to travel from anger through passion and down to the pit of despair, from which she was still trying to crawl.

Thrusting away the depressing thought, Anna reviewed her notes for her presentation. The tactic didn't work too well, since every page bore Evan's stamp. He had taken her words and expanded them, adding his thoughts, corrections and—dare she think it?—his charm. His style was vastly different from hers: less direct, more diplomatic. Yet somehow, they meshed. Why couldn't they weave their lives together like that? Dropping the papers to her lap, Anna looked up and stared blindly ahead.

She had to stop this.

She had to stop loving Evan McKenzie.

Closing her eyes against potential tears, she took a deep breath and held it as she counted to ten. Letting it out slowly, she regained composure. Choices had been made and now they all had to live with them. She would make it through this meeting, fly back home and enjoy the rest of her life without him. No one had ever died of a broken heart. They had just felt that way.

At the sound of her name, her eyes opened and she turned around in her seat again. Mimi and Ian waved from the back of the room as they worked their way up to the front. Anna was surprised to see so many people: nearly half the chairs were filled already. She set her paperwork on the adjacent chair, stood and hugged her brother and her friend when they reached her side.

"What are you doing here?" she asked.

"Full family force," Ian said with a smile. "If they don't grant us permission, Pop wants us all to rush the stage."

"Everyone's coming?" Anna asked, frowning.

"Pretty much." Ian ticked off attendees on his fingers. "Us, Jeannie and Charlie and their kids, Ma and Pop, Patrick, Kate and Kate's aunt Molly. Then there's most of the guys from the yard, the Greens and at least two dozen other neighbors and friends. You've got the house stacked in your favor, sis. Give 'em hell!"

Anna felt a swell of love for her family. "You did *not* have to come," she said, hugging them again. "But I'm glad you did."

"We're in this together, Annie." Ian kept his arm around her. "Anything you need, we're here for you."

"Thanks." The word wobbled a bit as it came from her

lips. Why had she moved three thousand miles away from these wonderful people?

The noise level in the meeting room had risen as they talked. Ian was right: the room was going to be full. She waved and smiled at her family and those she recognized from the boatyard or the neighborhood. A trio of commissioners now stood behind the table. They seemed oblivious to the crowd as they chatted with each other.

Patrick and Kate walked up and greeted them all.

"Ready for action?" Patrick asked.

"As I'll ever be," Anna said. She turned to Kate. "What, no Beth? I'm disappointed."

"The last thing we need is a toddler who's reached the 'terrible twos' a few months early." Kate shook her head in dismay.

"She's ahead of all her peers. We're so proud of her," Patrick said with a grin.

"You don't get the pleasure of her tantrums all day long."

"No, but I get the pleasure of yours after work," Patrick said, putting an arm around his wife and squeezing her to his side.

Kate threatened to slap him, then gave him a kiss. Watching them tease each other, Anna felt a pang of loneliness and envy.

"Everybody's here," Patrick said. "The whole family, except for McKenzie. I doubt he'll show up, since he's still on Pop's shit-list."

"He may be crazy, but he isn't stupid," Ian said.

"Too bad he's not *crazy* about me," Anna said with a rueful laugh.

An uncomfortable silence fell over the group, until Ian spoke up. "The thing is, Evan *is* crazy about you. He's just fighting it."

"Sounds like someone else I used to know. Doesn't it?" Mimi asked, nudging Ian with her elbow.

"Hey, I came to my senses," Ian said.

"Gave up a losing battle, you mean," Patrick said with a chuckle.

Ian shrugged, but his face lit with a grin. Anna glanced to the left, toward the doors. Her parents were greeting everyone they knew. She smiled as she saw Antonio throw his hands up in the air, then clap a man on the shoulders and kiss him on both cheeks. The Italian always came out when her father worked a room. Then, out of the corner of her eye, Anna caught a glimpse of a figure framed in the doorway. It was enough to stop her heart for a second and send a shiver across her skin.

Evan had come.

She felt a sudden burst of pride. What it had cost him to be here, she didn't know. But he had done it. He had shown up, even though he must know he was the last person her father wanted to see. He looked tired and weary, yet strong and handsome, too, in his dark blue suit with a tie in navy stripes, his hair brushed and gleaming. Everything she could want in a man.

But everything she would never have, too.

"Well, I was wrong," Ian said. "He is stupid." He put a hand on his sister's shoulder and gave it a consoling squeeze.

They watched Evan square his shoulders and step cautiously into the room, as if he expected someone to shoot him at any moment. As he edged his way through the crowd to a seat in the back, eyes and whispers followed his passage and more than one person glared at him.

Anna caught the moment that he saw her parents. His cool, stoic expression shattered for just an instant. She saw such grief and pain on his face that her heart ached for him. It hurt even worse when his quick glance took her in, standing together with her brothers and their wives. He looked away and Anna wanted to weep for him; he seemed so alone. But there was nothing she could do. He chose his path.

"Better grab a seat," Patrick said. "Before they're all taken."

Anna sank down onto her chair, weak and numb. Pulling her files back onto her lap, she kept her head down, eyes on the letters of the first page. The words themselves were illegible to her. Evan was not the only stupid one in the room. Her heart was just as foolish. It could not stop loving him. Maybe it never would.

ONE LOOK AT ANNA AND the sadness in her eyes was enough to make Evan crumble and almost back out of the room. He had to force himself to keep moving forward. Regardless of what they had said yesterday, Patrick and Ian didn't look happy to see him, either. Evan was pretty sure that Antonio and Elaine had not noticed him. Which was a good thing, because Antonio was likely to throw him out into the street. Not wanting to push his luck, Evan slipped into an aisle seat in the second-to-last row.

He had contemplated not showing up tonight. It would be the safest alternative. He knew he would not be welcome. Two things had gotten him to his car and underway. First was that Anna might need his help. She probably wouldn't *want* it, but he was not going to let Miriam Shermer sharpen her claws on her again. The second thing was that, even if they hated him for the rest of his life, he was going to do everything in his power to secure Antonio and Elaine's future. He owed them that much.

With any luck, things would go well. He could sneak out before it was over and disappear into the night. In the meantime, he hunched over in the chair and put his head in his hands. It ached with the accumulated pressure of three sleepless nights and a new, deep understanding of his own immutable flaws.

Those standing around him began sitting down, too. Just when he thought he was out of danger, a familiar voice called his name loudly. He looked up: Elaine Berzani was headed his way. Conversation nearby ceased and everyone turned to look at Evan. He froze for an instant, then steeled himself to stand. He would face this on his feet, like the man he had failed so miserably to be.

As Elaine approached, Evan watched her intently. Her face was lined not with anger or vengeance, but with sadness. Elaine stepped closer and he braced himself. He deserved anything she chose to throw at him. When she kissed his cheek, then put her arms around him, Evan was so shocked he simply stood there, unable to move. His heart thudded in panic mixed with hope. Slowly, fearing he was dreaming, he returned her embrace. Elaine patted him on the back and Evan held her tighter.

"I'm so sorry," he whispered into her hair, his voice a hoarse rasp.

"Yes, dear. I know," she said, drawing back to gaze up at him. Tears rolled down her cheeks and she dabbed at them with a handkerchief. Evan felt a renewed rush of shame and anger with himself. Even though he knew Elaine cried for the smallest reason, he was sorry to know that this time *he* was the cause of her tears.

Evan was not surprised when Antonio came and stood beside his wife. Elaine was too soft to chastise Evan, but her husband would have no such qualms. As a boy, Evan had learned that lesson well. Ready to receive his rightful punishment, Evan released Elaine and turned to meet the older man's stern gaze. Antonio's dark eyes, so much like Anna's, drilled into Evan's mercilessly.

"We must talk, you and I."

Evan swallowed. "Yes. Mr. Berzani, I—"

"Hey! What is this 'mister' business?" Antonio scowled at him. "Am I no longer 'Pop' to you?"

The question struck Evan's core and bewildered him. He did not know how to answer. "I screwed up. I made a mess of Anna's life."

"Yes, you have done that," the older man agreed sharply. "And you have done the same for your own, I think."

Evan could only nod.

"Well, this is why we must talk. You and I, we can straighten things out, make sure this child gets what it needs."

"Not now, dear. We better get to our seats." Elaine tucked her hand into the crook of her husband's arm. "I saved three up front next to the kids."

"Perfetto!" Antonio rubbed his hands together triumphantly. "They cannot say no to the whole Berzani family."

Evan looked at them, unsure he could believe any of what he had just heard. Was he forgiven? Or were they just being kind? Or maybe this was some elaborate fantasy he had dreamed up.

As if he sensed the younger man's confusion Antonio stopped, put a hand on Evan's shoulder and shook him a little. "You are *family,* Evan. Nothing can change that."

Evan searched the man's eyes and saw the truth. There was disappointment and hurt there, but love shone more brightly. The knowledge dazed him. When Elaine tugged at his arm, he followed unresistingly.

"Hurry up, dears," she said. "The chairman is seated."

Seconds later, Evan found himself sitting in the front

row, a line of Berzanis stretching out to his right and behind
him. His head whirled as he tried to understand why Elaine
and Antonio still loved him. How could it be that he could
hurt them so much and still be part of their family?

The gavel fell, the meeting started, but Evan barely paid
attention. Anna rose. He had a clear view of her as she took
her post at the podium. She began to speak. Her words were
a murmur of sound in his ears, their meaning indistinct, but
her face fascinated him. She was so beautiful, so vibrant
and alive. He had missed her unbearably over the past
two days. How was he going to endure a lifetime without
her?

Evan glanced down the line of seats and saw a family
that stuck together through the hard times. Generations
supporting each other: living, loving, fighting, working.
Together. They were a wonder to behold. Even more wonderful was the realization that he was a part of it. Evan
looked at Patrick and could almost hear him saying again
how no one got a guarantee. Marriage was work, but it
was the best, most satisfying kind. Evan could also hear
Ian asking him to look deep into himself and discover his
love for Anna. They were his best friends and his family
and, for better or worse, he belonged to them. Both he and
Anna.

Elaine, sitting beside him, took his hand. She was holding Antonio's hand on her other side. She shot him a glance
full of forgiveness, gave him a reassuring squeeze, then
turned back to her daughter's speech. He loved her like a
mother. He loved Patrick and Ian like brothers. Antonio he
might very well love more than his own father.

Looking over at Anna again, Evan admitted that he
loved Elaine and Antonio's daughter, too. What he felt for
her was deeper and wider than his love for any of the other
Berzanis. He wanted her in his life for now and for*ever*,

even more than he wanted this family. Acknowledging this truth was like shedding a terrible weight he had carried for too long.

Evan realized that he wanted to take the chance he had never allowed himself before. He wanted to be a true part of the family with Anna and their child. Without intent or forethought, they had laid the foundations. Now he knew he wanted their child to have the parents he had not been born with, but had been lucky enough to find when his own failed.

It occurred to Evan that his reasons for avoiding marriage were based on the worst that could happen. But what if it didn't? What if the best happened instead? What if he reached out and took what he wanted and they were both happy? Evan had always claimed to be his father's son, but now he wondered which father held the most sway over him, Antonio Berzani or James McKenzie? A leopard never changed his spots, and neither did Evan McKenzie. But whose spots was he wearing?

Evan heard Anna begin her summation. He had written most of it himself. He might be biased, but he thought she was doing well. He looked at the table of commissioners and tried to read their minds. Except for Miriam Shermer, they appeared so stoic or even bored that he could not tell. Anna concluded, thanking the committee for allowing them a special session and for considering their request.

The chairman turned to his cohorts and asked if there were any questions or concerns. There were none. Except for Miriam Shermer. Her scathing questions and sarcastic criticisms were nearly a repeat of last week. This time, Evan's temper boiled over before Antonio's. He was *not* letting her take a piece out of Anna—never again. It was time for the gloves to come off. Standing, he went to the podium.

Anna was in the middle of showing the commission a graph of noise levels in the new development, assuring them that they would be far less than the boatyard now produced. Miriam was already making negative noises, sending huffs of irritated breath through her microphone, triggering feedback. Evan nudged Anna aside gently. With a look of shock, then annoyance, she stepped back.

"Mr. McKenzie, it is not time for comments from the audience," the chairman said stiffly.

"Mr. Chairman, as you know, I'm an applicant for this project," Evan said, raising the microphone to his level. "In fact, most of the folks in this room tonight are, too."

"What is your point, Mr. McKenzie?" the chairman asked.

"My point is that we're all wasting our time. *These* people all want the work to go through and *you* would have approved it if Miriam Shermer hadn't raised such a stink. A stink that she knew was bogus from the start."

A few loud agreements and some groans came from the audience. The chairman banged his gavel. "Order! Order!"

"Quiet everyone," Evan said sharply into his microphone. As the crowd quieted, Evan looked directly at Miriam Shermer. "I'm sorry I hurt your niece, Miriam. I didn't love her, but I should have been kinder in letting her know that. My only excuse is that I was confused about the woman I *do* love. If it's any consolation, I managed to hurt her at least as much as I hurt Kippy."

The whispers in the room rose to a buzz. The chairman rapped for quiet again. Evan looked at Anna and saw her eyes were filled with tears. She had put a hand to her trembling lips.

Before turning back to face the panel, Evan took Anna's hand and pressed a gentle kiss to her palm. It was a simple request for her forgiveness, for spurning the love he had never deserved in the first place and now wanted more than anything in life. She blinked and gazed at him with wonder and confusion.

"Miriam, I understand why you want to repay the suffering that I caused Kippy," Evan continued, looking at the older woman again, but keeping Anna's hand tightly gripped in his own. "I know that's probably why you've picked apart our project. Family takes care of family. I didn't realize what that meant before tonight. I do now. I hope you'll realize that this project is *about* family, too."

Evan paused and scanned the faces in the first two rows. "The Berzanis built the marina and boatyard from virtually nothing into a place where people come to work and to play. They will bring the same dedication and thoughtfulness to this new development, making it just as much a part of the community, if not more. I hope my own children will be involved in it. I hope they will share part of the legacy the Berzanis started with their love. Miriam, please accept my apology."

There was a smattering of applause.

Miriam Shermer was not pleased, an unhappy scowl on her round face. "Very heartfelt, I'm sure. Is that all, Mr. McKenzie?"

"No, it isn't. Tonight was our second appearance before this committee. You did not need to grant us that chance, but you did. We thank you all. But I need another second chance. Tonight, I want to start over with Anna Berzani."

Evan turned and looked at Anna. Her eyes were dark with an emotion he couldn't name: anger, embarrassment, terror, nausea? She simply stood there. He could see a fine tremor run through her, but she remained silent. Evan swallowed, his heart sinking. The worst was happening. He had pushed her too far, left his plea too late.

Then the most wonderful thing happened. Anna rose on tiptoe, slipped her arms around his neck and pulled his lips to hers. Her kiss held love and forgiveness in abundance. Evan clutched her tightly to his heart, offering his own promises for their future. The cheers, laughter, whistles and catcalls from the audience went unheeded. Even the chairman left his gavel alone.

Then Patrick called out, "Ask her to marry you again, McKenzie!"

"I should leave that until after the vote," Evan said, lifting his mouth from Anna's and looking deep into her eyes. "I don't want to hold things up any longer."

A ripple of laughter filled the room as the microphone picked up his words.

"Coward," Patrick said loudly.

"I advise you to make it quick, Mr. McKenzie," the chairman said. "This is a planning-commission meeting and we still have work to do." But he was smiling, as were three other commissioners. Even Miriam's sour look had softened.

Evan looked down at Anna. She was blushing, but her eyes shone clearly and unmistakably with her love. Slowly, holding her gaze, he released her from his arms and stepped back a pace. He dropped to one knee before her. Lifting her hands to his lips, he kissed each one tenderly.

"I asked you this once before, but this time, I ask from my heart." Evan looked up at her intently. "Anna Berzani. Will you marry me?"

"Yes, Evan McKenzie." Anna's voice was shaking. "*Yes*. I will."

Evan rose and swept her into his arms, his lips finding

hers again in an instant. The room erupted in cheers, but he barely heard them. His own heart was drumming in his ears, blocking out all other sounds. His heart and Anna's beating together, forever.

Epilogue

As Evan reached the top of the stairs, a faint wail sounded from the back of the condo. The closer he got to it, the louder it became. Anna appeared in the doorway of their bedroom. Her red curls spilled over the shoulders of the oversize white shirt she wore. She had requisitioned it from his closet, as usual. When she was large with pregnancy, she had gotten in the habit of wearing some of his clothes. He never complained. Why would he when she looked small, sweet and infinitely sexy in them.

"He was asleep when I put him down ten minutes ago," she said, frowning in the direction of the nursery. "He's been fed and changed, too."

"I'll get him," Evan said, handing her the two glasses he was carrying. He dropped a kiss on her lips. "He's probably just upset that the Ravens lost again."

"Like father, like son," she said with a grin.

Evan went to fetch his son. Looking down into the crib, he saw four-month-old Anthony James McKenzie blinking up at him owlishly. "What's up, little man?"

Scooping the baby up in his arms, Evan carried him across the hall, through the bedroom and out to the deck where Anna sat. Dropping onto the love seat beside her, Evan settled Tony onto his chest. Taking the glass of wine that Anna handed him, he sipped, sighed contentedly, then set it aside. It was another perfect September evening: warm, not too humid, with a bit of a breeze. The sun had dropped behind the trees on the opposite bank of the inlet, bringing a mellow light to the water in front of them.

The baby squirmed a little, working to lift his head. As usual, the gleam of the gold chain around Evan's neck had attracted his attention. A little starfish hand reached out and seized the prize. The four buttons, one white, the others pale green, slid on the chain and squirted out of his grasp.

"He goes right for them every time," she said with a soft smile.

"A man who knows what he wants."

"*That's* not his father's trait," Anna teased.

"Oh, I knew what I wanted," Evan said in lazy protest. He ran his gaze over his wife in a slow, sensual appraisal. "I just didn't think I deserved it."

A blush colored Anna's cheeks. Her eyes warmed to molten chocolate and Evan knew she felt the same rush of desire he did. He slipped his free hand through her hair and cupped her neck, bringing her in for a long, luscious kiss. Anna leaned into him, her body curving against his, setting his pulse pounding.

A sudden indignant cry forced them apart.

"He doesn't like being ignored." Anna's voice was husky.

"Just like his mother."

When Anna laughed, Tony smiled the toothless, lopsided grin that thrilled his grandparents. He wriggled in Evan's arms, making a chortling sound of glee. Anna buzzed her lips against the side of his neck and he squealed with delight.

"He's going to be awake for a while. I can tell."

"That's okay. We can wait." Evan laid his head back against the cushions.

"Anticipation," she said, lifting her glass of juice and smiling at him over the rim.

His body tightened. He remembered that night as well as she did. Soon, they would replay those wonderful moments and build new ones. Just as they had been doing since that night back in October when he finally came to his senses and proposed.

It never ceased to amaze him how satisfied he was with his new life. Why had he ever thought living alone was a pleasure? Anna had moved back to Crab Creek, despite Evan's protests and offers to relocate to San Francisco. She wanted to be near her family as much as he. When her boss, Carl, learned that he might lose his second-favorite architect, he proposed that she open an east-coast branch of the company and become managing partner. After its nearly unanimous approval by the planning commission, the Berzani boatyard had become the fledgling company's first project.

They had married two days after Christmas and eagerly planned for Tony's arrival. Evan had been at Anna's side when their son made his debut in late May. Now they traded off baby care with his ecstatic, doting grandmother, Elaine. Though Evan's own mother and father were distant figures in Tony's life, Evan knew his son would get all the love he ever needed in Crab Creek.

Anna put her drink down and looked out at the water.

"What are you thinking?" he asked.

"Remember that first day I came here? To work on the project?"

"Are you kidding? It's etched in my memory forever." He shook his head with a laugh. "I remember hearing you on the second floor. I knew *exactly* when you stepped inside my bedroom. It was all I could do to not come up and keep you here for the rest of the day."

"I only went about a foot inside!" A flush colored her cheeks.

"Annie, an inch would have been enough," Evan said with a chuckle.

Anna joined his laughter and Tony gurgled again. She let him grab her finger and tug on it. Her eyes on the baby, she continued, "I stood in the doorway and imagined you drinking wine with some woman who was wearing your shirt. It was horrible."

"Annie, I—"

"I'm not asking about your past, Evan," she said gently, her gaze meeting his. He could read the love in her face as clearly as if she had spoken the words. "I just wanted it to be me, out here with you."

"You know, Annie," he said softly, slipping his free arm around her and pulling her close. "I don't think you saw my past that day."

Nuzzling her face into his neck, she asked, "What do you mean?"

"I'm sure that woman I was with had red hair. And if you'd looked closer, I think you'd have seen a baby with them."

"You're much better at seeing the future than I am," she whispered, snuggling against him.

Surrounded by his family, Evan's heart was full. Tony cooed his satisfaction at having his two favorite people so close. Evan kissed the downy head, then Anna's tempting lips. She laid her head on his shoulder and they were quiet for a while. Tony seemed to sense the contentment and settled at last, relaxing onto his father's chest. His squirming ceased and he yawned.

Evan tightened his hold on the two most important

people in his life. Anna was wrong; his view of the future was still foggy. But the visibility was improving. He had Anna and Tony; with them, his future shone bright with endless potential. All he had to do was dare to reach out for it through the mist. Even now, it surrounded him, warm, loving and loved. His home, right here in his arms.

* * * * *

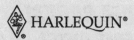 **HARLEQUIN®**

COMING NEXT MONTH

Available September 14, 2010

REQUEST YOUR FREE BOOKS!
2 FREE NOVELS PLUS 2 FREE GIFTS!

HARLEQUIN®

American Romance®

Love, Home & Happiness!

HAR10R

HARLEQUIN®

A *Romance*

FOR EVERY MOOD™

Spotlight on

Heart & Home

Heartwarming romances
where love can happen
right when you least expect it.

See the next page to enjoy a sneak peek
from Harlequin Superromance®,
a Heart and Home series.

*Enjoy a sneak peek at fan favorite Molly O'Keefe's
Harlequin Superromance miniseries,*
THE NOTORIOUS O'NEILLS, *with*
TYLER O'NEILL'S REDEMPTION,
*available September 2010
only from Harlequin Superromance.*

Police chief Juliette Tremblant recognized the shape of the man strolling down the street—in as calm and leisurely fashion as if it were the middle of the day rather than midnight. She slowed her car, convinced her eyes were playing tricks on her. It had been a long time since Tyler O'Neill had been seen in this town.

As she pulled to a stop at the curb, he turned toward her, and her heart about stopped.

"What the hell are you doing here, Tyler?"

"Well, if it isn't Juliette Tremblant." He made his way over to her, then leaned down so he could look her in the eye. He was close enough to touch.

Juliette was not, repeat, *not* going to touch Tyler O'Neill. Not with her fingers. Not with a ten-foot pole. There would be no touching. Which was too bad, since it was the only way she was ever going to convince herself the man standing in front of her—as rumpled and heart-stoppingly handsome now as he'd been at sixteen—was real.

And not a figment of all her furious revenge dreams.

"What are you doing back in Bonne Terre?" she asked.

"The manor is sitting empty," Tyler said and shrugged, as though his arriving out of the blue after ten years was casual. "Seems like someone should be watching over the family home."

"You?" She laughed at the very notion of him being here for any unselfish reason. "Please."

He stared at her for a second, then smiled. Her heart fluttered against her chest—a small mechanical bird powered by that smile.

"You're right." But that cryptic comment was all he offered.

Juliette bit her lip against the other questions.

Why did you go?

Why didn't you write? Call?

What did I do?

But what would be the point? Ten years of silence were all the answer she really needed.

She had sworn off feeling anything for this man long ago. Yet one look at him and all the old hurt and rage resurfaced as though they'd been waiting for the chance. That made her mad.

She put the car in gear, determined not to waste another minute thinking about Tyler O'Neill. "Have a good night, Tyler," she said, liking all the cool "go screw yourself" she managed to fit into those words.

It seems Juliette has an old score to settle with Tyler.
Pick up TYLER O'NEILL'S REDEMPTION
to see how he makes it up to her.
Available September 2010,
only from Harlequin Superromance.

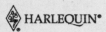